"You don't listen, do you?"

Cutter was speaking in that authoritative, rankling military tone again. She wasn't under his command. "I listen just fine." She started to march away.

Cutter grabbed her arms and tugged her around to face him. "You're a kindergarten teacher. You know kids better than I do. Secret surveillance and invasion without detection are my areas of expertise. I'm not risking either of us getting arrested—or killed—because you're too stubborn to listen to reason."

"So it's your way or not at all?"

"In this case."

He wasn't going to budge. His attitude was arrogant, determined. And unequivocally protective. She wanted to lash out at him, but the truth was she'd never felt more safe and turned on in her life.

JOANNA WAYNE

COWBOY COMMANDO

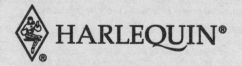

HARLEQUIN®

TORONTO • NEW YORK • LONDON
AMSTERDAM • PARIS • SYDNEY • HAMBURG
STOCKHOLM • ATHENS • TOKYO • MILAN • MADRID
PRAGUE • WARSAW • BUDAPEST • AUCKLAND

I'd like to offer my gratitude to the brave military
men and women who sacrifice so much to protect our freedom.
And a hug and heartfelt thanks to the people who love them.

Recycling programs
for this product may
not exist in your area.

ISBN-13: 978-0-373-69390-0
ISBN-10:   0-373-69390-7

COWBOY COMMANDO

www.eHarlequin.com

Printed in U.S.A.

ABOUT THE AUTHOR

Joanna Wayne was born and raised in Shreveport, Louisiana, and received her undergraduate and graduate degrees from LSU-Shreveport. She moved to New Orleans in 1984, and it was there that she attended her first writing class and joined her first professional writing organization. Her first novel, *Deep in the Bayou*, was published in 1994.

Now, dozens of published books later, Joanna has made a name for herself as being on the cutting edge of romantic suspense in both series and single-title novels. She has been on the Waldenbooks bestselling list for romance and has won many industry awards. She is a popular speaker at writing organizations and local community functions and has taught creative writing at the University of New Orleans Metropolitan College.

She currently resides in a small community forty miles north of Houston, Texas, with her husband. Though she still has many family and emotional ties to Louisiana, she loves living in the Lone Star state. You may write Joanna at P.O. Box 265, Montgomery, Texas 77356.

Books by Joanna Wayne

HARLEQUIN INTRIGUE

955—MAVERICK CHRISTMAS
975—24/7
1001—24 KARAT AMMUNITION*
1019—TEXAS GUN SMOKE*
1041—POINT BLANK PROTECTOR*
1065—LOADED*
1096—MIRACLE AT COLTS RUN CROSS*
1123—COWBOY COMMANDO†

*Four Brothers of Colts Run Cross
†Special Ops: Texas

CAST OF CHARACTERS

Linney Ringley Kingston—Her quest to get justice for her friend leads her into danger and back into the arms of a past lover she's never been able to forget.

Cutter Martin—He'll protect Linney no matter the cost to his own life or to his heart.

Al Kingsley—Linney's ex-husband.

Amy Colley—The police report says she died in an accidental drowning.

Aurelio—Foreman at the Double M ranch.

Dr. William Gibbons—A man with ties to Amy Colley.

Dane Colley—Amy Colley's husband, a homicide detective with the GHPD.

Edna Sears—Amy Colley's mother.

Goose Milburn—An old friend of Cutter's and a Houston police detective.

Julie Colley—Amy Colley's three-year-old daughter.

Merlee Martin—Cutter's aunt who lives at the Double M ranch.

Saul Prentiss—Police chief.

Wesley Evans—Dane's partner in the homicide division of the GHPD.

Chapter One

"Welcome home, cowboy!"

Cutter Martin stopped just inside the door and waited for his pupils to adjust from the bright sunshine to the dim lighting of the bar and grill. Even after they had, it took a few minutes for him to spot the lean male frame propped on the barstool a few yards away.

Tom Porter. He hadn't seen the guy in years. Would have been fine with Cutter if he'd gone a few more. The mood he was in right now was not suitable for company, especially not Tom's. He waved anyway and made his way to the nearly empty bar.

"Not quite home," Cutter said, sliding onto the barstool next to Tom, "but close."

"Houston's a hell of a lot nearer to Dobbin than Afghanistan was."

"When you put it that way." Odd thing was Dobbin, Texas didn't seem like home anymore, either. There had been nights of sleeping on the hard ground in insect-infested forests that made the Double M Ranch loom like heaven in the back of his mind.

Now he was back in the States and the ranch was just wide open spaces. He figured he'd gone too deep into enemy territory and the military lifestyle to go back to his ranching roots. Not that he'd ever been much of a rancher. It was bronc riding on the rodeo circuit that had driven him in his younger days.

The bartender wiped a spot of moisture from the counter in front of Cutter and slapped down a paper napkin. "What can I get you?"

"Scotch on the rocks. Make it a double."

"I saw your picture in the *Houston Chronicle* last month," Tom said. "I been meaning to look you up ever since then. That was quite a hero's welcome you got."

"Yeah." Cutter nodded and looked away, hoping that would end the hero talk. He hadn't been any more a hero than every other frogman he'd served with.

Unfortunately, the bartender must have overheard Tom's remark. He paused as he served Cutter's drink. "Say, you're that Navy SEAL fellow, aren't you? The one who personally killed twelve of the enemy after you and your buddies were ambushed."

"So they told me. I wasn't counting at the time."

"Cool, man. I thought about becoming a Navy SEAL. My girlfriend didn't like the idea of my getting shot at, though."

Cutter studied the guy. Early twenties, hair a little too long, tattoos all over his arms like blotchy skin. Big enough, but no muscular definition. Cutter wondered if he'd last a day in BUD/S. Basic Underwater Demolition/SEAL training was twenty-six weeks of grueling preparation for what lay ahead for the few who saw it through.

"You must be glad to be home," the bartender continued. "Bet it was even worth getting shot in the leg to get out of the war zone."

As if on cue, Cutter's left thigh started to throb and his irritation level climbed. The bartender wasn't the first to assume he must have hated his time in the service. They were dead wrong. It was trying to adjust to life without the rugged edges that was taking the fight out of him. He didn't seem to fit in civilian life half as well as he'd fit in with his SEAL team.

He picked up his drink and downed half of it before setting the glass back on the table. Fortunately, by that time another customer had snagged the bartender's attention. Now he only had Tom to contend with.

Tom grabbed a handful of peanuts from the bowl near him, spilling a few down the front of his plaid cotton sport shirt as he dropped them into his mouth. "Are you planning to get the ranch up and running again now that you're back? I hear your aunt sold most of the stock."

Actually, she'd sold everything except her favorite horses. That was part of his adjustment problem—not that it had come as a surprise. It just hadn't quite hit home until he saw the empty pastures.

She'd asked Cutter before she'd auctioned off the herd. He'd told her to go ahead. At the time he hadn't been planning to leave the SEALs for years. The land was still there. Livestock could be added at any time.

Merlee loved her newfound freedom. At seventy-five, she was ready to travel and do some of the things his uncle Hank had never been interested in.

"They say you can't go home again," Cutter said, when he realized that Tom was still staring at him, waiting for an answer.

Tom nodded. "I know what you mean. Too quiet out in Dobbin for me. No action and nowhere to find any. I'm in waste management now, right here in Houston."

"Sounds like a winner." Cutter finished his drink. "Good to see you. I've got to run, though."

"Too bad. I was thinking if you didn't have plans, we might grab a bite to eat together. Catch up on old times."

"Maybe another day."

"Yeah, right. I'll give you a call. You in the book?" Tom asked.

"Yeah, in the book. Look me up."

Cutter pulled some bills from his pocket and left them on the bar, more than enough to cover the price of the drink and a tip. He didn't look back as he pushed through the door and back into the humidity of a hot June afternoon.

He had another interview scheduled, this one at a new car dealership out on I-45. He made a quick decision to blow it off. Selling cars just wasn't going to cut it. Not that he had a clue what would.

He missed the danger, missed knowing that every decision was crucial, missed feeling the heat of the enemy breathing down his neck even when he couldn't see them. Most of all, he'd lost the feeling that what he was doing made a real difference.

Houston wasn't a walking town, but Cutter couldn't bring himself to crawl back into the new black Chevy pickup truck he'd left parked in the lot. He stopped by it just long enough to shed his tie and sports jacket and toss them into the backseat of the double-cab. Then, rolling up his sleeves, he headed down Montrose Boulevard.

Breaking a sweat felt good. He covered the blocks fast in spite of his slight limp, turning onto Westheimer and then onto a dozen more streets he never bothered to check the names of. Cars whizzed by him. A black man on a bicycle almost ran him over. A guy walking a pair of poodles walked by Cutter without glancing his way.

A young woman in a thin summer dress that hugged her perky breasts and swung from her narrow hips walked out of a coffee shop on his right. She caught his eye and smiled at him invitingly. He considered stopping to see how far her invitation went, but decided against it. She was about ten years too young for him and likely a lifetime too innocent.

He kept walking, past cafés that were no more than holes in the wall emitting odors of peppers and chilies and frying tortillas. Past upscale dining spots with white-shirted valets parking Mercedes and BMWs.

He was in an eclectic area of shops, restaurants, and aging houses infiltrated by sleek new townhomes, all practically within the shadows of the downtown skyscrapers.

It was dark when he ended up back at the bar, and the parking lot was full. He started to go in for another drink but decided to head back to the tiny claustrophobic condo where he was staying. Two rooms, unless you counted the closet-size bath. A living/kitchen area and a bedroom. Fortunately, there were lots of windows.

Merlee had bought the property a few years back when Hank had first been diagnosed with cancer and was undergoing chemo. It was near the hospital and had eliminated the long commute during that already stressful time.

She'd decided to keep it after he died and now she and her friend Josie used it when they wanted a few days of city living. Culture, she called it, though the theater and symphony attendance was rivaled by shopping and baseball. Merlee was a rabid Astros fan.

She'd given Cutter the key to the condo when he'd started searching for employment. He'd have to take the job hunt more seriously tomorrow. Deal with more applications.

Skills: Hand-to-hand combat. Smelling out the enemy. Putting his life on the line.

None of them looked particularly good on a résumé.

There was a light on in the condo when he pulled in to his parking spot. He didn't remember leaving it on, and it couldn't be Merlee or Josie. They were off on an Alaskan cruise. He'd driven them to the airport himself.

His instincts for trouble checked in. He hesitated at the door. Interesting odors wafted out. Garlic. Onions.

The voices coming from inside were even more interesting. The male was undoubtedly George Strait singing "All My Exes Live in Texas." The female singing along with a definite lack of enthusiasm and totally off-key was anybody's guess. Except…

No. He was imagining things.

Cutter opened the door, unlocked now, though he was sure he'd left it locked this morning. He stepped inside. There was definitely a woman in his kitchen and singing along with his CD. He headed that way.

"Honey, I'm home."

"Cutter."

No mistaking the voice when it called his name. His body tightened. His stomach flipped. A second later Linney Gayle Ringle stood in the doorway. Her red hair was caught up in a knot at the nape of her neck, but more than a few tangled curls fell over her cheeks and danced about her forehead.

He gave in to the initial spicy thrill of her, letting his gaze scan her shapely body before reining in his natural instincts and reminding himself of the misery that had stemmed from their last encounter. Not to mention the fact that she was now a married woman.

She looked up at him from beneath her thick lashes, her emerald-green eyes as bewitching as ever, though the sparkle he remembered was shadowed.

"God, you look good, Cutter, much better than that newspaper photo."

To say she looked good would be the understatement of the year. She was dynamite. Too hot too handle. Nothing new there.

"Nice to see you, too, Linney. Now, care to tell me why you broke into my condo?"

"I didn't. Merlee gave me a key."

"That explains it." He let his gaze scan her body again, then wished he hadn't. Her breasts were perky little mounds that pushed against the thin cotton T-shirt that scooped just low enough to show a hint of cleavage. The white shorts hit midthigh, showing off the perfectly tanned legs. Legs that had once wrapped around him while—

He fought the stirrings back into submission before he reached really dangerous territory. "So why are you here, or do you chase after every guy who gets his picture in the paper?"

"Just the cute ones."

She walked over, rose to her tiptoes and gave him a peck on the cheek. "We're friends, Cutter. I wanted to welcome you home."

There was a tenseness about her that made him sure that wasn't the whole story—not by a long shot. "You can do better than that, Linney."

"Not in present company." Linney put her hand out and Cutter spotted the little girl who'd just stuck her head around the counter that separated the living area from the kitchen. The preschool-age child walked over and scrunched behind Linney's shapely hip before stealing a sheepish glance at Cutter.

So Alfred and Linney had a daughter. Might even have a house full of kids. "Where's big Al," he asked, "or is he going to jump out next?"

"You heard about the marriage?"

"Word gets around."

"All the way to the Middle East?"

"Just the big stuff."

"Alfred and I are divorced."

That he hadn't heard. "Is this where I'm supposed to say I'm sorry?"

"Are you?"

No and yes. It was easier to resent the both of them if they were living their idyllic life in the world of the rich and modestly famous. "Divorce is tough on kids," he said, knowing it was the most honest statement he could offer.

"Alfred and I didn't have children."

So there was a new man in her life. And still Linney was here, in his condo, the spitting image of the woman who'd starred in thousands of his unsolicited erotic fantasies over the last six years. But only after he was sound asleep and too out of it to remember that she'd walked out on him without so much as an adios.

"Look, Cutter, I know it's in bad taste to just let myself in, but I wasn't sure when you'd be home and I didn't want to keep Julie out in the hot sun."

"How did you know I was staying here?"

"Your aunt Merlee called last week and told me. She thought I should give you a call and welcome you to Houston."

"I didn't know you and Aunt Merlee were such good friends."

"We talk at the symphony during intermission, mostly about you. Our seats are only two rows apart."

"Nor did I know you were a fan of the symphony."

"There are lots of things you don't know about me."

"Apparently. Is this story going somewhere, Linney? Because I've had a really long day, and I'm not up for entertaining."

"You don't have to get in a huff, Cutter. Just tell me where you keep your extra sheets and blankets and I'll make Julie a bed on the sofa."

"Whoa! This is not a hotel."

"I know, but I need a favor. One night." She managed a strained smile. "And I cooked dinner. There's pasta with red sauce. No meat. You didn't have any—or much of anything else except beer and moldy cheese."

"I wasn't expecting company."

"Just for one night, Cutter. I promise. We won't put you out."

"I only have one bed."

"Julie can sleep on the sofa."

Which would leave the one bed for him and Linney. It was hard enough controlling his libido standing in the same room with her. Fat chance he'd be able to do it with her stretched out next to him between the same pair of sheets.

"You can't stay here." His command came out a lot harsher than he'd intended. Julie started to cry.

"Now see what you've done." Exasperation and a tinge of desperation tugged at her voice and expression.

Linney dropped to the sofa, took the small child in her arms and started rocking her back and forth. "Cutter didn't mean to frighten you, sweetheart. He's glad you're here. He loves little girls. Tell her, Cutter."

"I adore them. Linney, we have to talk."

"Right, as soon as Julie's asleep, but that will take a little longer now that you've upset her."

Cutter still had no clue what was going on, but the chances that he was going to sleep alone in this apartment tonight were growing slimmer by the second. If the vibes of anxiety Linney was emitting weren't at frightening levels, he'd insist she go to a hotel.

But there was more going on than Linney had admitted in front of the child, and there was no way he could just toss her out if she were in some kind of real trouble. His gut instinct was that she just might be.

"Put Julie in my bed," Cutter said. "The sheets are fresh. The cleaning woman was here today. You can sleep with her and I'll take the couch."

"Thanks, Cutter. I knew I could count on you."

Their gazes met and he had that same crazy sensation he used to get when he was parachuting into a hostile environment with no clear means of escape.

"Just for tonight, Linney. Don't even think of unpacking a suitcase or finding a spot for your toothbrush."

"No luggage," she admitted. "No toothbrush, either. I was kind of hoping you'd have an extra for your sleepover guests."

"I don't have sleepover guests." At least he hadn't until now.

Cutter watched Linney walk toward the bedroom with the young child clutching her hand. He followed the pungent odors to the range and lifted the lid. A deep red sauce was simmering in the pot.

He dipped a spoon into it, blew on the hot liquid, then hesitantly sampled the sauce. Not half-bad. It surprised him that the wife of a man as wealthy as Al Kingston actually cooked.

And she'd become a mom. In none of his fantasies on the cold, hard, mountain earth had he ever pictured her standing over a kitchen range or tucking a golden-haired little girl into bed. Now here she was in the flesh and the surprises just kept on coming.

He was setting the table when Linney rejoined him. She went to the refrigerator, opened the door and took out a couple of beers. "Can I offer you a drink?" she asked.

"Only if it comes with an explanation as to why you're entertaining me in my own kitchen. And don't revert back to the friendship scenario. That won't cut it."

"You're not going to like it."

"I figure that's a given." He opened the beers and pushed hers across the table to where she'd dropped into one of the padded wrought iron-and-wood dining chairs.

She toyed with her beer, finally taking a tiny sip. "You're the only one I have to turn to."

"What about Julie's father?"

She shook her head.

"I don't want to be pulled into something between you and your husband."

"There's no husband, Cutter. There's just me and Julie. That's why I need your help."

"Why me?"

"Everyone in Dobbin has been talking about you. You've won medals for your bravery. You're used to danger and not afraid of anything."

Except spending the night in this house with Linney. "Cut to the chase. What have you got yourself and your daughter into?"

"Well, you see, that's just the thing, Cutter. Julie's not my daughter. I've kind of... Well, it's just that..." She threw up her hands in a display of frantic frustration. "I sort of kidnapped her."

Chapter Two

"You sort of kidnapped her? What is that supposed to mean?"

Linney tried to stay calm. "I didn't set out to do it. The woman at the day-care center called and said Julie was crying hysterically. I went to check on her."

"Why did the center call you instead of her parents?"

"They tried to reach her father. He didn't answer his cell phone. Amy—her mother—had put my name on the emergency caller list so the woman who manages the center called me."

"If you're on the list, then how is this kidnapping?"

"I said 'sort of' kidnapping. You have to pay attention, Cutter."

"It would be easier if you didn't talk in riddles. The father must have called you by now to see where his daughter is and when you plan to bring her home."

"He hasn't."

"Then this is simple. Just take Julie home."

"It's not quite that simple."

His eyebrows arched again. "Because…"

"Keep your voice down. You'll wake Julie."

"She's already asleep? What did you do, drug her?"

"Don't be ridiculous. She's exhausted and she's been through a terrible ordeal over the last few days."

"A sort-of kidnapping will surely help that."

"Sarcasm under fire is not the mark of a hero, Cutter Martin."

"I never claimed to be a hero and we're not under fire. Not yet, anyway."

Linney flashed what she hoped was a persuasive look. "Would you just sit down and let me explain?"

"I like standing, and I don't see how anything you will say can justify a kidnapping—or even a sort-of one."

Linney studied Cutter. He looked different than he had the last time she'd seen him. Older, harder and, if possible, even more ruggedly handsome. Then, desire had fired in his dark eyes. Tonight his gaze seared into hers accusingly.

His five o'clock shadow was pronounced, his face a mix of taut planes and angles, his muscles strained and pushing against the white cotton dress shirt. The white dress shirt didn't fit the image she'd carried of him for the last six years, not even with the top two buttons undone and the sleeves rolled up to just below his elbows.

The rest of him fit the image perfectly. The lean, hard body. The tanned skin. The thick locks of dark hair falling across his forehead giving him a devil-may-care look and a sexiness that wouldn't quit.

Linney took a deep breath, exhaled slowly, then pushed her back against the slats of the chair. "Julie's mother drowned last Friday. Amy Colley. You may have read about it in the newspaper. It happened in Green's Harbor. That's a small town on the bay about twenty miles south of Houston."

"Yeah, I know where Green's Harbor is. And I read about the accident. Her husband came home from work and found her floating in their backyard swimming pool."

"That's what *he* said. It's not what happened."

Cutter's eyebrows arched. "Oh?"

"He killed her."

"By *he,* I assume you are talking about the husband?"

"Yes, Dane Colley. Amy's husband."

"And also Julie's father?"

She nodded.

"I suppose you have proof of your accusation."

"I don't have hard evidence, if that's what you mean. But I know he did it."

"So now you're psychic?"

"This isn't a joke, Cutter."

"I'm not laughing." His eyes narrowed and his jaw clenched. "Didn't I read that Dane Colley is a homicide detective?"

"Yes, and that's the worst part of all this. He knows how to play the system and he's got friends in all the right places. They'll take him at his word and there won't be a real investigation into the murder. He'll just kill my friend Amy and get away with it—unless someone stops him."

"Did you talk to the Green's Harbor Police Department about your suspicions?"

"I tried. I gave the clerk a statement and he said I'd hear from one of the detectives. That was two days ago. I've called several times since then as well. No one's called me back. I also called the news department of several of the local TV channels. They told me they'd need more than groundless suspicions to run a story."

Cutter walked to the refrigerator and retrieved a couple more beers. He opened them both and set one in front of Linney. "Only two left," he said. "I'm not sure that will get us through this explanation."

"You asked for the facts."

"I'm still waiting for the main one. Why is the daughter of the recently deceased mother and the homicide-detective father sleeping in my bedroom?"

Linney pushed back from the table. "Don't you get it?

I can't get through to the police via normal channels, but if they suspect I've kidnapped Julie, they'll have to contact me. And if the media gets involved, all the better."

Cutter took a huge gulp of the cold beer before finally straddling one of the kitchen chairs. He stretched his left leg in front of him and massaged the thigh.

She knew from what Merlee had told her that he'd taken two bullets in that leg. She wondered if the stress she was causing him was making the wounds ache. She hoped not, but it couldn't be helped.

"You're not making a lot of sense, Linney. If there's a beginning to this story, I suggest you start there."

The beginning? Linney had no clue how far back the roots of the murder actually extended, but her first suspicion about Dane Colley went back to the day she'd met Amy. It had been the faculty's first day of school last September. The fading bruise on Amy's right cheek had caught Linney's attention during the principal's introduction of new staff members.

It had brought back bitter memories of the one and only time Alfred had slugged her. She'd packed her bags that night, left his overpriced, gaudily grandiose mansion in River Oaks and never returned.

The punch had done what years of unhappiness and feeling like the pseudo-princess of a bogus furniture kingdom couldn't. It had knocked some sense into her and freed her to file for divorce.

Linney hadn't asked Amy about her bruise that day, but she had asked her about several subsequent ones over the next few months as she and Amy developed a friendship. Amy had always made flimsy excuses—until last week.

"Are you going to talk or not?"

The impatience in Cutter's voice pushed Linney to find a place to begin. "Amy and I both work at the Green's

Harbor Kindergarten and Early Learning Center," she said, deciding basic background was all he really needed to know. "I'm a teacher. Amy's a paraprofessional."

"When did you start teaching?"

"Two years ago, right after I left Al. This was Amy's first year and she's come to work with bruises on her face and arms too many times to count."

"Did she say her husband had caused them?"

"No. I think she was too embarrassed to admit it. She always came up with some ridiculous story about falling over a rake in the garden or walking into an open door."

"Yet you seem sure he's to blame?"

All too sure. Linney took a sip of the beer. "Amy called me last Thursday and asked me to meet her at the café on Bay Drive for coffee. It was the first time I'd heard from her since school had let out three weeks earlier for summer vacation and I was really looking forward to seeing her."

"What happened?"

"When I arrived, she was already sitting at one of the outside tables near the water. The first thing I saw when she looked up was a violently purple bruise and a ball of swollen flesh beneath her right eye. That time when I asked her about it, she admitted that Dane had punched her."

"Did she say why?"

"Does it matter why?"

"Call me curious."

"He'd tried to reach her on her cell phone and couldn't."

"Sounds brutal."

"It sounds criminal," Linney said, "because it is. Amy told me she was afraid of him. She'd made up her mind to leave him, even though he'd threatened to kill her if she ever tried it."

If Linney had suspected for a second what was going

to follow, she'd have begged Amy to run away that very day. But who could foresee murder?

"And this was last Thursday before Amy Colley drowned on Friday?"

"Right. Dane must have found out she was leaving and made good on his threat."

"That's a big assumption, Linney."

"Men kill their wives. I hear about cases like that all the time on those TV crime documentaries. And those are just the ones who get caught."

"Maybe so, but thousands of women leave abusive husbands every year. Very few of those husbands resort to murder."

"Then I guess Dane's the exception."

"Have you seen him since Amy's death?"

"I saw him at Amy's funeral, but didn't get a chance to speak to him."

"When was that?"

"Two days ago, on Monday afternoon."

"The same day you went to the police."

"Right. I attended the funeral with several of the other teachers from the school and more than one commented that Dane didn't look like a man bereft because he'd just lost his wife. He didn't shed a single tear. That added a lot of fuel to my suspicions."

"You can't accuse a man of murder based on the flow of his tears, or the lack thereof."

"I'm not basing my accusation on any one thing. But when you put it all together, it's obvious that the drowning was no accident."

"I wouldn't go that far, but I'd agree that the drowning raises a few questions. What I don't see is how you think being arrested for kidnapping is going to improve the situation."

"Do you have a better idea?"

"Almost anything is better than that, unless you're ready to go to jail to prove your point."

"Dane killed Amy," Linney said. "I'll do whatever it takes to make sure he doesn't get away with it. I thought you of all people would understand that."

"All I understand is that you are in big trouble, Linney. How long have you had Julie?"

"Since four-thirty."

Dane checked his watch. "It's after eight now. I can't believe Dane hasn't tried to get in touch with you."

"He doesn't have my cell-phone number, and I haven't been back to my house."

"He's a cop. He could get your number."

"Then I don't know why he hasn't called. Maybe he's just glad not to have his daughter around."

"More likely, every cop in this part of Texas is out looking for you."

Cutter reached over and laid his hands on top of hers. The touch was casual, almost incidental, yet it affected her in a way she hadn't expected. It was as if his strength and support made her feel more vulnerable.

She was swimming in dangerous waters, not only in the situation with Julie but in her own conflicted emotions regarding Cutter. She wasn't the naive, gullible, nineteen-year-old coed she'd been six years ago. She didn't need another relationship on a fast track to nowhere—no matter how hot and thrilling their brief fling had been.

"I can see where you're coming from, Linney, but kidnapping a detective's kid is over-the-top. Even if some high-priced lawyer keeps you from going to prison, no school board is going to hire a teacher who's been accused of kidnapping."

She hadn't considered that, and she loved teaching.

Cutter stood and walked back to the counter, leaning his backside against it and staring at her as if she were some disobedient private he was about to dress down.

"I have a friend in the Houston Police Department, Linney. Goose Millburn and I were on the same SEAL team for my first two years in the service. I'd trust him with my life. In fact, I have on several occasions. I'd like to run the situation by him and get his take on this."

"His take will be that I return Julie and we'll be right back where we started—with Dane getting away with murder."

Cutter pulled his cell phone from his pocket and started punching in numbers.

"What do you think you're doing?" she demanded.

"Calling Goose."

Linney's temper flared. "I didn't agree to that."

He turned away, but kept punching in numbers. Linney jumped on his back and tried to wrestle the phone from his hand. Her right foot hit the table and the two empty plates went crashing to the floor. Her fingers stayed wound around the phone.

A whimper came from the doorway. When Linney looked up, Julie was standing just inside the kitchen, clutching in her tiny hands the teddy bear she never slept without. Her eyes were wide with fear. Linney let go of the phone and slid from Cutter's back.

"We're not fighting, sweetheart. We're just playing around, aren't we, Cutter?" She kissed him on the cheek to prove her point to the bewildered and frightened tot.

Cutter's arm closed around her and his hand splayed around her shoulder. He was merely playing along with her attempt to reassure Julie, but something warm and unexpected zinged along Linney's nerve endings.

She jerked away. She'd had six years to get over her meaningless sexual marathon with Cutter. Whatever she felt now was just some kind of poorly timed reflex brought on by her own desperation.

Julie crept closer, her stuffed toy held tight against her chest and her gaze cast toward the floor.

"I guess we don't have to make the call this instant," Cutter said. "Get Julie settled again, and then we'll eat. No use letting good pasta go to waste."

"Thanks." It was merely a reprieve, but that was better than a phone call to the cops. It would give her time to think and decide what she wanted to do. She figured she had about half an hour before she had to make her next move.

She didn't have a clue what that would be.

THEY BARELY SPOKE through dinner. What else was there to say? Cutter had given his ultimatum. Call Goose or take Julie home. Arguing with him would be a waste of time, and Linney wasn't about to beg.

She tried to force down a few bites of the food, but it stuck in her dry throat. Cutter, on the other hand, went back for seconds. Apparently, his impatience and irritation with her had little effect on his appetite.

She glanced at her watch, the extravagant diamond-studded Rolex Al had given her for their second wedding anniversary. She'd never liked it. "It's almost time for the nine o'clock news. I'd like to see if they mention a kidnapping."

"You finish eating. I'll turn on the TV." Cutter took his plate to the kitchen, rinsed it beneath the spray of the faucet and left it in the sink before flicking on the set.

Linney tensed, as the blond female anchor looked grimly into the camera to deliver the night's teaser.

"A double homicide in Green's Harbor has left three children orphans and set off a massive manhunt for two unidentified suspects who held a family hostage for nearly two hours this afternoon."

No mention of a kidnapping or an Amber Alert. So Dane hadn't reported his daughter missing. And he hadn't tried to call her. It didn't add up.

"And this just in…"

Linney's attention spiked again.

"Income tax fraud charges are expected to be filed tomorrow against furniture magnate Al Kingston. Stay tuned for these and other important happenings from the Houston area."

Linney had just stood to carry her own plate to the sink. The fork she'd balanced on the edge clattered and fell to the tiled kitchen floor, spraying her blouse with red sauce on the way down. She grabbed a paper towel and dabbed, spreading the stain.

Cutter rushed to the sink, wet a clean dish towel and came to her rescue. He pressed the cloth to the stain, a spot right over her right breast. The water seeped into the fabric outlining the nipple and revealing its puckered tip.

The air turned steamy. "Just leave it," she murmured, backing away.

Her cell phone rang, startling her and making her jump so that she tripped over the leg of her chair. Cutter caught her and steadied her. "Are you all right?"

Not even close, but she nodded. The phone kept ringing.

"Don't you think you should get that?"

"It's probably someone calling about Al. I don't want to deal with that."

"It could be Dane."

She went to the living area and grabbed the purse from her handbag, checking the caller ID. "Margie Clemens. She's a teacher at the kindergarten. She probably just caught the news about Al."

Linney sank to the sofa to catch the rest of the news. Cutter propped himself up on the arm of the overstuffed occasional chair near the window. There was no mention of the kidnapping.

"Check your cell phone," Cutter suggested at the next commercial break. "See if you have a message from Dane that you missed earlier."

She checked. There was none.

"This smells rotten," Cutter said. "Surely Dane's gone to pick up his daughter by now and heard that she left with you. Or is the day-care center open all night?"

"No, the last pickup is seven o'clock sharp. Not complying can get you replaced with another child from their waiting list. I've had to pick up Julie before when Amy was tied up and Dane was working. That's why I'm on the emergency contact list."

"Being on the list doesn't mean Dane doesn't have an APB out on you by now. I'll call Goose. He'll know where to go from here. By the way, did you have any idea your ex was involved in tax fraud?"

"Not a clue, but I'm not surprised. Al's whole life was about acquiring and spending money. The pending charges may explain why we still don't have a property settlement, though. He may think he's going to need his ready assets for attorney fees."

"You've been divorced two years and you still don't have a property settlement?"

"We've been separated two years, divorced one. My attorney says we're close to a property settlement, or at least we were before this came up."

"Okay. Forget Al for now. I'll call Goose. Stay calm this time. You know it's the only sensible thing to do."

And just like that, Cutter was taking over, calling the shots and ignoring the fact that he was helping a man get away with murder. And it wasn't as if she were putting Julie in danger.

A plan started taking shape in Linney's mind. Not

perfect, but better than seeing Amy's killer live to abuse and kill again.

This one's for you, Amy. If you have any influence up there, try to keep me out of jail, will you?

"GUESS IT'S TIME for Julie and me to hit the road."

Cutter looked up as Linney came back from the bedroom where she'd gone to check on Julie. She'd freshened up a bit, put on some lipstick and returned the escaping tendrils of red hair to the clasp at the nape of her neck.

"I'd like to go with you," he said.

"No. I made a mistake in coming here, but I'm not going to compound that by involving you any more than I already have."

"You're in good hands with Goose."

"So he says. He's meeting me at the precinct. I'll give him a statement of my suspicions about the drowning not having been an accident and he'll go with me to take Julie home unless he's gotten in touch with Dane by then. If so, he'll have Dane pick her up. Either way, if there's any confrontation between Dane and me, it will all be a case of police record."

"Goose means it when he says he'll follow up with the GHPD on your suspicions of murder."

"I'm sure he does."

"But you're not convinced that it will do any good?"

"Green's Harbor is out of his jurisdiction."

Which could be why Cutter had this sinking feeling that he'd let Linney down. "I'll carry Julie to the car for you."

"Thanks. She's heavier than she looks, but try not to wake her. I'd rather she remain asleep until I get her home."

Cutter tried to be gentle, but he had no experience with kids. Julie's head rolled and then settled against his chest. He felt an unexplained tightness. Poor kid. She'd lost her mother. Now her only parent was a man Linney was convinced was a murderer.

Holding Julie like this, he could almost understand Linney's determination to see justice done. But having Linney go to prison for kidnapping was not the way to do it.

Linney led the way to her car, a silver BMW sports convertible that was waiting in a visitor's slot on the third floor of the parking garage.

"Nice wheels."

"A present from Al just before I left."

He'd love to know more about that breakup, or maybe he wouldn't.

Linney opened the back door and he placed Julie inside, fastening the seat belt around her. She squirmed and then let her head drop to the cushioned headrest of her booster seat without ever opening her eyes.

Cutter shut the back door and walked around to the driver's door. It was standing open, though Linney was already behind the wheel and fitting the key into the ignition.

"Are you sure you won't change your mind about my going with you?"

"I'm sure. I'll be fine, Cutter. You know, you really should visit your aunt Merlee more. And get some groceries in your house."

He leaned in to kiss her good-bye. Not smart, but he wasn't feeling particularly smart right now. She turned so that his lips brushed her cheek as she shifted into Reverse. Not a lot left for him to do except close the door and watch her drive off.

He did, then slumped against the back bumper of the red pickup truck that was parked right behind him. She waved and smiled as she turned toward the exit, then gunned the engine and took off.

Feeling emptier than he'd felt since leaving the service, Cutter started back to the elevator of the parking garage, then decided to take the stairs to his fourth-floor condo. Before the accident, he would have run them. He'd be able to again soon, but never with the speed and agility he'd had when his body had been at its peak of performance.

The metal steps rattled on impact, the sound echoing around him as he ascended the lighted stairwell. The sound took him back. The clanking became Russian-made tanks in the distance rattling their way toward him and his team.

They'd been on a rescue mission, one that sane men would have called off when that kid had spotted them in the heavily forested terrain and took off running. One kid was all it took to alert a small army of the Taliban's men.

They could have stopped him with a bullet. Not one of them ever would have. He was just a kid.

But they were not leaving their captured buddy in the hands of the enemy. It was against the code of the SEALs and everything they lived by.

Linney must feel a similar commitment to get justice for her friend Amy. He knew she wasn't convinced that Goose could make that happen. Yet she hadn't seemed that upset when she'd driven off, certainly not as irate as she'd been when he'd first insisted it was the right thing to do.

Cutter came to a screeching halt. What the hell had he been thinking? Linney wasn't going to meet Goose. She was on the run again. It was an idiotic act that would likely land her in prison for the best part of her life.

Cutter spun around and raced back to the garage, this time to his parking spot. He burned rubber in his haste to exit. Not surprisingly, there was no sign of Linney's car by the time he pulled onto the side street that fronted his complex. She had at least a five-minute head start and that could put her anywhere.

He turned right at the corner, toward Interstate-10, the most probable escape route if you wanted to get out of town quickly. East would take him into downtown Houston. West would take him toward San Antonio.

Neither choice bode well for spotting her. The traffic on I-10 was always crowded with eighteen-wheelers and gas-guzzling SUVs. Her low-slung sports car would be difficult to spot among them.

Not that it was a sure bet she'd taken the freeway. She could have decided to stay on back roads. There were dozens of possibilities there.

The traffic light at the corner switched from yellow to red. Cutter slowed, then spotted a car exactly like Linney's pulling out of a service station on the opposite corner.

He waited for the traffic to clear the intersection, then sped through the red light and passed two cars on the right to put him almost directly behind Linney as she turned onto the entrance ramp to I-10, going west, not toward the precinct where she was supposed to give a statement to Goose.

She accelerated, switching lanes quickly, jumping right in between two speeding vehicles. He kept her in sight until some jerk with a suicide wish cut right in front of him on his Harley. Stamping on the brake and swerving to the right, Cutter just managed to keep from colliding with the biker and the babe clinging to him like plaster.

Kidnapping Julie was a crazy stunt. Impulsive. Irresponsible. Coming to him tonight had probably been just as crazy, but then he seriously doubted that Linney had spent six years trying to get over their five nights of fun and games and sexual fireworks.

Cutter had grown up fast in Afghanistan and Iraq, learned the difference between instinct and impulse, discovered how one misstep could cost a life. He knew to pick his battles wisely. At least he thought he had until Linney had shown up and in trouble.

Linney switched lanes again, this time two at a time. She was going to exit, a sudden decision, he guessed. The car behind her switched lanes as well. There was no siren or flashing lights, but Cutter had a strong hunch that the nondescript black sedan held an undercover cop.

Linney pulled into the exit lane. The car behind her stayed on her tail. Cutter swerved in front of a pickup truck and exited a couple of cars behind the sedan.

Linney turned right at the first traffic light. The sedan pulled into a service station. Cutter breathed a little easier. He was certain it would go better for Linney if she returned Julie before there was any police confrontation.

She took a quick left, crossing a set of railroad tracks and turning onto a road that ran beside it. The area grew instantly darker as they left the illumination of streetlights.

A tall fence dominated the side of the road nearest the tracks. There were scattered businesses on the other side. A machine shop. A brake and muffler repair center. A white brick building with a sign promising the best prices in Texas on body work. All closed.

Theirs were the only two cars on the isolated road, and he seriously doubted that Linney had a clue where she was going. He increased his speed, narrowing the space between them as she rounded a curve.

He'd pull up next to her and let her know he was onto her scheme. Maybe she was having second thoughts. With luck, she'd be nervous on this dark road and desperate enough by now that she'd stop and listen to reason.

No such luck. Linney accelerated, leaving him behind. He'd spooked her by getting so close and now she was driving dangerously fast.

Cutter caught a glimpse of movement ahead, then

watched a car that resembled the same dark sedan that he'd thought was tailing Linney on the freeway. It pulled out from a deserted lot and onto the road in front of Linney.

The car was driving slow and inching toward the center of the road, straight at Linney. She slowed and headed for the shoulder to avoid a collision if he swerved too far into her lane.

Cutter's apprehension swelled. If the driver of the approaching car kept coming at the same angle, he'd swipe the side of Linney's car—or worse. The car kept coming, but now the barrel of what appeared to be a machine gun jutted from the window.

Son of a bitch. This was a setup. The man was going to gun her down and there was no time to stop him.

In seconds, she'd be dead.

Chapter Three

The adrenaline rush hit the way it had hundreds of times before, producing an instantaneous honing of all Cutter's instincts and training.

Cutter lay on his horn, then veered to the left, crossing the center line and ramming the right-front fender of the shooter's car just as the crack of gunfire thundered in the night.

His breath burned in his lungs. His move had been worse than risky. It was damn near suicidal. But better than doing nothing while Linney's head was blown off at close range.

The shooter's car raked the side of Linney's, then sped away. Linney's sports car skidded out of control. She careened off the right shoulder, kicking up dirt and dry leaves before lurching down an incline and slamming into a ditch. Miraculously, the sports car didn't flip.

Cutter skidded to a stop on the muddy shoulder, grabbed his flashlight from the glove compartment and raced to Linney's vehicle.

His heart was racing as he peered through the window. The airbags had inflated and were pushed against Linney's chest so that all he could really see was her face. Blood trickled down her left cheek but there was no visible gaping wound.

"Were you hit?"

"Cutter?" Her eyes were wide, riveted to his, though even in the moonlight he could see that her flesh was ghostly white. "How did you get here?"

"Lucky move." His breath scorched his lungs. "Are you okay?"

"Yeah, I think so. Nothing hurts, but someone just took a potshot at me."

He gasped huge gulps of air and the burning in his chest eased to the point that he could breathe without searing pain.

Julie started to wail. Cutter opened the back door and slipped into the backseat to check on her. Linney managed to extricate herself from the airbag and tumble over the back of the seat, squeezing in between him and Julie. She cradled Julie's head in her arms.

"It's okay, baby. I'm right here with you."

Cutter did a quick visual scan for injuries while Linney tried to calm her. There was no sign of a bullet wound. "She appears okay," he said.

"Thank God! Does anything hurt?" Linney cooed.

Julie wrapped her arms around Linney's neck and clung to her as if she were afraid her protector would disappear into the darkness if she let go. "I want my mommy."

"I know, sweetheart."

Linney's voice dissolved into a quake that felt like shrapnel exploding in Cutter's gut. Linney had come to him for help and he'd practically kicked her out of the condo.

Chances that the attack was random were slim to none. She'd been ambushed. Was that why Dane hadn't called? Had he killed his wife and then tried to kill Linney to silence her and her suspicions? If he had, he'd risked killing his own daughter as well.

But then he wasn't expecting interference from Cutter. A sharpshooting cop would have been able to place the bullet exactly on target at that speed and distance.

Cutter crawled from the car and did a quick assessment of damage to the vehicle. It would require towing and bodywork, but there were no bullet holes. Apparently, the shooter had missed his target altogether. But if Cutter hadn't been here...

He swore under his breath as fury raced through his veins like a roaring river. He scanned the area. The road was deserted. No sign of headlights. No sign of trouble, but that didn't mean this was over.

Let down your guard for an instant and the enemy gained the advantage.

This enemy was already armed, while he wasn't. And the enemy had known exactly where to find Linney, had likely followed her when she left Cutter's condo. There was only one valid explanation for that.

With the help of his flashlight, Cutter searched every inch of the car, working quickly, and making a call to Goose as he did. He explained the latest developments.

Goose let fly a few expletives Cutter hadn't heard since leaving the Navy.

"Were you able to get in touch with Dane?" Cutter asked.

"I left a message at the phone number the GHPD gave me. He hasn't called me back. The clerk on duty said he's on the scene of a major crime and has been for hours. He promised to let Dane know that his daughter's with Linney Kingston and that she's fine."

"Does that mean there's not an APB out for Linney?"

"Nope. I'm assuming the day-care center got the word to Dane that Julie was with Linney. He must be okay with it."

"Then I guess we're covered on that score."

"As long as Linney cooperates in reuniting father and daughter at the earliest opportunity."

"I'll see that she does."

"I suggest you all go to bed and try to get some rest for now. I know I am. But be careful."

"Yeah."

Cutter finished checking out the car. When he was done, he stuck his head through the open back door. "We need to get out of here. I'll help you get Julie to my truck."

"I can't just leave my car here."

"You won't be driving it out of that ditch. It's practically standing on the front bumper. I'll call a tow truck."

"I can't go to the cops, Cutter. You saw what—" Linney stopped herself before blurting out Dane's name. She buried her face in Julie's soft hair, kissing her on top of the head. "You saw what he's capable of."

"I saw what someone's capable of. Now let's get moving. We can decide on an operational plan later."

"Forget a plan," Linney said. "I just need a ride back to my house in Green's Harbor. I'll handle things from there."

Linney stayed entangled with Julie, but turned her face so that she was looking at Cutter. Her disheveled mass of red hair was loose now and bouncing about her shoulders. Arbitrary curls rested against her bloody cheek.

Her chin was jutted at a defiant angle and she had a determined strength in her stare that the more youthful Linney of six years ago would never have been able to pull off. Unfortunately, she was as damn irresistible as ever.

"I'm not leaving you," Cutter said.

"You saved our lives. You've done enough."

It sounded reasonable, but Cutter knew that the instant he'd spotted that gun pointed at Linney's head, his choice in this was gone. He could no more walk away now than he could sprout wings and fly or whisper some kind of chant and have his old life as a Navy SEAL back.

"I don't want to make any rash decisions about what to do next. I like a clear plan of action before I engage. But I'm not leaving you, so get in the truck before the lunatic returns and I have to save you again."

She shifted, peering out the back window as if she thought his prediction would hex them and conjure up headlights. When she didn't see any, she picked up Julie's teddy bear and tossed it to him. "I'll carry Julie if you'll get her booster seat and grab my handbag out of the front seat. And remember, you asked for us."

Mere moments later, they'd abandoned Linney's car in the ditch and were heading back in the direction they'd come from. He'd hold off on telling her of his conversation with Goose until Julie was asleep or they were alone.

"Why did you choose this road to nowhere?" he asked.

"I've been on it before with Al. He has a warehouse a couple of miles farther down. The company outgrew the facility, but Al held onto it. Said he couldn't get enough for it to make selling it worthwhile."

"Tell me you weren't planning to hide out there like some criminal on the run."

"I don't owe you any explanations."

Which meant that was exactly what she'd planned to do. "Do you have a key to the warehouse?"

"No, but I could probably figure out the alarm code to keep it from going off. Al's not the most creative guy when it comes to passwords and codes."

"So you were going to break in to one of your ex's properties and hide out with Julie instead of meeting with Goose."

"Desperate situations call for desperate measures."

Desperate measures didn't appeal to Cutter. He liked his risks spelled out and alternate courses of action in place in case he met resistance. As a SEAL, he'd never accepted failure as an option. He definitely wouldn't now.

When he reached an intersection, he took a road less traveled, a narrow FM road that headed north, as a plan of sorts started forming in his mind. Somehow the claustrophobic condo with one bed and no weapons didn't seem conducive to strategy planning or keeping Linney safe.

"How do you feel about Dobbin?" he asked.

"You can't bring your aunt into this."

"She's on an Alaskan cruise."

"What about her foreman? Doesn't he still live on the property and take care of the land and her horses?"

"Aurelio is still there, but I can't see what difference that makes. He has his own house." The more Cutter thought about it, the better the idea of crashing at the Double M sounded.

So it was back to Dobbin, Texas, and the ranch. And back to Linney and an almost guaranteed one-way trip to heartache.

CUTTER STOPPED at the metal gate.

"I'll get it," Linney offered, already opening her door to jump into action.

The weathered condition of the rectangular, hardwood Double M sign suggested that it had endured years of Texas thunderstorms and blazing summer heat. It clattered a dubious welcome as Linney jumped from the truck.

The iron scrolls in the gate seemed to be staring at Linney, as taunting as an evil grin carved into a Halloween pumpkin. Even the ranch didn't want her here, causing trouble for Cutter.

She unlatched the gate and swung it open. The headlights of Cutter's pickup truck pushed into the darkness, illuminating the rutted dirt road in front of her.

She knew from past visits that the road led through acres of fenced pastureland before banking what counted as a hill in this part of Texas and then veering off toward a huge pond and the sprawling ranch house.

She'd visited the ranch dozens of times before, albeit never with Cutter. As a teenager she'd come here for hayrides with laughing church youth groups or for the mini-rodeos or 4-H events that Hank and Merlee had hosted.

Good folks, people said of his aunt and uncle, the words not nearly conveying their wealth or the influence the couple had held in the small rural community.

Hank can close a deal on a smile and a handshake, and you can stake your life that he'll keep his word.

Linney's own dad had said that too many times to count and she knew that Hank Martin had bailed him out financially on more than one occasion.

Once the vehicle rattled across the cattle gap, she closed and latched the gate and scrambled back into the truck. "I'm surprised your uncle never blacktopped this road," she said as they dodged a deep rut. "When there's a heavy rain, the road must be almost impassable."

"Uncle Hank believed a ranch should feel like a ranch and that cows didn't need paved roads. And he always had four-wheel-drive vehicles."

"Your uncle was one of a kind."

"He would say he was just from good Texas stock."

"Merlee must miss him a lot."

"I'm sure she does, but she stays upbeat and busy with her gardening and church activities. And traveling with her friend, Josie Watts. I think they've cruised every place there's a tour. This is their second time to Alaska."

"What do you think she'd say if she knew you were bringing Julie and me here?"

"She'd tell me I'd better not let anything bad happen

to either one of you." Cutter slowed as a large deer stepped into the beam of his headlights. The buck stood motionless, head high, his impressive rack pointing skyward until they were almost upon him. Only then did the magnificent creature turn and run away.

She wondered if the deer sensed danger the way she sensed it now that someone had tried to kill her. No, not someone. Dane. It had to have been him, though she couldn't imagine how he'd found her so quickly. More disturbing was the fact that he'd opened fire on her with Julie in the car. Now she was expected to just turn the child over to the murderous lunatic.

She checked to see if Julie was still asleep. Satisfied that the toddler was in dreamland, Linney shifted and turned to face Cutter. "Coming here was probably a major mistake."

"You tell me."

"I'm serious," she said, keeping her voice low so as not to wake Julie. "Dane could show up any minute. He must have someone tailing me. How else would he have known I'd be on that road?"

"With this." Cutter took a black gadget the size of a half dollar from his shirt pocket and tossed it into her lap. "It's a tracer, the newest model, highly efficient."

"Where did you find this?"

"Attached beneath the back bumper of your car."

"Dane must have planted it there right after I made that complaint to the police department," Linney whispered. "I'll bet the clerk went straight to him with my suspicions."

"He probably thinks of Dane as a reliable cop."

"No wonder no one's called me back. Dane probably tossed the report."

"We're going on a lot of assumptions here. It's

possible the good detective hasn't seen the report, didn't plant the tracer and wasn't tonight's sniper."

"Oh, puh-leeze!" She checked again. Julie was still fast asleep. "He's behind all of it. He's so arrogant he thinks he can get away with anything. He would have killed me, then stopped and rescued his daughter. End of his problems."

"Aren't you forgetting that the day-care center attendant knows Julie left with you today?"

"But they don't know that I didn't drive her home."

Cutter wrapped both hands around the wheel and stretched, grimacing a bit as he rubbed his left thigh. He was probably seriously regretting his offer of help about now. Maybe he figured that six years involved in some of the Middle East's most dangerous counterterrorism operations was enough heroism for one guy.

She lowered the window a few inches and took a deep breath, letting her lungs fill with the fresh, country air. Smells of pine mixed with wild verbena and the sweet magnolia Merlee had planted along the drive.

Julie stirred in the backseat, and Linney raised the window quickly before the sting of wind had her fully awake. Hopefully the three-year-old would sleep through the night.

"The ranch house is just ahead," Cutter said. "I'm sure the freezer will be fully loaded but I'm not sure about perishable provisions."

"We'll make do until morning," Linney said, suddenly hit with mind-numbing fatigue. "Then we'll need milk for Julie. She'll need clothes, too."

Cutter rounded the last curve and brought the truck to a jerky stop in the driveway. He yanked the gear into park and turned to face her, his muscles taut and his jaw set at the same unyielding angle as when he'd told her she had to go to the police.

"I don't know what you're thinking, but this is not a permanent arrangement."

"But—"

"No buts. The minute we hear from Dane, Julie goes home."

"Fine." She jumped out of the car before she said something that would really piss Cutter off. She opened the back door to get Julie.

"I'll carry her inside," Cutter said, handing Linney his key ring with an oversize bronze key protruding. "You get the door."

"You're sure no one's here?"

"I'm sure Merlee's in Alaska."

Cutter unbuckled the seat belt and lifted Julie. She squirmed, raised her head, then let it fall to his broad shoulder. His hand splayed across her back. She looked even more petite in his strong arms, Linney thought. And Cutter looked...

Linney swallowed past a disturbing lump that swelled at the back of her throat. He looked strong and protective. Yet gentle. The image was incredibly seductive and not one she needed to carry into a house where she'd be spending what was left of the night with Cutter.

This was all about getting justice for Amy. Even a hint of the passion that had burned inside her six years ago could screw up her mind and make this even harder than it already was. Far better to just stay aggravated with him.

She opened the door, stepped inside and flicked on the light. The feel of the house wrapped around her like a silken cocoon. It was Merlee to the core. Comfortable. Overflowing with warmth, from the hooked rug to the large overstuffed chairs upholstered in a muted plaid the color of autumn hay.

"We can put Julie in the guest bedroom at the end of the hall," Cutter said. "There's only a twin bed, but it's next to the master suite and it will be easy to hear her if she wakes during the night. The other bedrooms are upstairs."

"I want her near me."

"I planned on you taking the master suite."

"Where will you sleep?"

"I'll bunk down somewhere if I get tired. But nearby. You'll be safe, so try and get some sleep. And by the way, there's no APB out on you. Dane's working a case, probably the one we heard about on the evening news. So obviously he's fine that Julie's with you, at least for tonight."

"When did you hear all that?"

"I talked to Goose while I was checking out your car. I didn't mention it then because Julie was awake."

So that's why he didn't believe that it was Dane who'd fired at her. But if not Dane, then who? Someone he'd hired? Or just another dirty cop? Danger might come from a dozen directions, but she wouldn't back off. Amy deserved justice.

Still, Linney doubted she'd get much sleep tonight.

CUTTER STOOD on the back porch of the house staring into the darkness. No night goggles the way he'd had on nights like this in the Middle East when he'd peered into pockets of danger that lurked behind every tree.

Tonight there was just a Texas moon, its silvery light filtering through the pines and painting shadows that danced in the slight evening breeze. But inside the house where he'd grown up, mere feet away, the woman whose image had haunted him night after night for the last six years was showering and getting ready to spend the night under his roof.

He'd told himself he was over her, that the skyrockets that had lit up his life for those five days and nights of lovemaking had never been as fantastic as they seemed. It was just that they followed on the heels of the endless days of BUD/S training.

Nice theory. Too bad that seeing the machine gun pointed at her head had blown the hell out of it. He'd make certain he wasn't stupid enough to let those uncontrollable desires take hold again.

But there wasn't a chance he'd walk away while she was in danger. Even if she went to the police or the FBI or hired a dozen bodyguards, he wouldn't be able to retreat from the situation until he knew she was safe.

Not that danger had ever deterred him.

Like that night in Afghanistan when he'd dropped from the helicopter with two other team members. They'd carried their full packs as they'd climbed the steep grade to the spot where Henry had last been heard from.

Sweat had dripped from Cutter's body until he was soaking wet as they'd tramped and cut their way through the heavy underbrush where one wrong step could have sent them plunging to their death.

The difference was that Cutter had understood the danger then. The threat against Linney made no sense at all. If Dane had killed his wife and covered his tracks well, which he would surely have known how to do, then why risk killing Linney just because she'd made a useless trip to the police station?

A piercing ring broke his concentration. Not his cell phone, so it was either someone calling Merlee or Linney. He hurried through the back door and found Linney's phone on the counter.

He checked the ID. Dane Colley. Ringing phone in hand, Cutter rushed down the hall to the master bedroom that Linney was using and knocked on the door.

"What is it?"

"You have a call from Dane."

The door flew open, but Linney didn't make a grab for the phone. Instead, she just stood there, wearing a white T-shirt that she must have pulled from Merlee's closet. The shirt fell off one shoulder and barely skimmed her private area.

The sight of her like that affected Cutter like a streak of lightning, all fire and hot desire. He pushed the phone into Linney's hands.

"Answer it."

Finally, they might find out what was going on in Dane Colley's mind.

Chapter Four

"Linney, it's Dane Colley. I'm sorry to wake you."

"You didn't."

"How's Julie?"

"She's asleep."

"Good. I'm really sorry not to get back to you sooner, but I've been on a hell of a case. I didn't even get the message from the day-care center that Julie was upset until I was on my way to pick her up at closing time. Somehow I let the battery on my cell phone run out of juice."

"They called me when they couldn't get you. Julie was crying hysterically. They didn't know what to do with her."

"That's what they said. Amy's drowning has been incredibly hard on her. On both of us. I hadn't planned to go to work at all, but I was going crazy at the house. And my depression was making it even worse on Julie."

Linney all but gagged on his fake grief and lies. She knew he'd not only killed Amy, but had tried to kill her tonight to shut her up. This was all a sick game to him.

"I really appreciate your helping out with Julie. She misses Amy so much and doesn't understand why her mother doesn't come home. I can't bring myself to tell her she never will."

Using Julie in this way made Dane a hundred times more evil. Anger erupted inside Linney, rolling in her stomach like churning rot. Struggling to control the venomous accusations she longed to hurl at him, she counted to ten. Still, civility didn't come easily.

"I tried to call you earlier," Dane continued, "but no one answered at your house. I wasn't worried. I knew you'd take care of her."

"I have." *Even when you shot at me.* "She's sleeping now, and I'd hate to wake her."

"I'll pick her up in the morning, then. I hope I haven't put you out too much. I called as soon as Wesley dropped me off here at the house and I got the message to try you at this number."

So this was how it was going to be. He had his alibi in place for the attempt on her life tonight. If she accused him of shooting at her on a deserted road in Houston proper, it would only make the rest of her claims to his guilt in the drowning seem less credible.

Linney looked up and saw Cutter's eyes boring into hers. He stepped closer and put a supportive hand on her shoulder. She put her hand over the phone. "He's playing nice," she whispered. "Says he'll pick up Julie in the morning."

"Tell him you'll bring Julie home in the morning. I'd like a chance to look around inside his house."

She nodded reluctantly. This was starting to feel like she was using Julie as a pawn. Now that she'd had more time to think about it, the kidnapping idea would have done the same thing.

"Why don't you let me drop her off? I have a few errands to run anyway."

"Okay, but I need her here by nine. I've agreed to let

Amy's mother's take Julie home with her for a few days and she's driving in from the Woodlands to get her."

Linney took a deep breath, but the air she inhaled seemed icy when it hit her lungs. She was dealing with a killer, making arrangements with him as if they were old friends when she knew the depths of his malice.

"I'll have her there before nine."

"Thanks."

The connection went dead. Linney went weak, her head seeming to swirl with the effort required to talk calmly with Dane. She shuddered and Cutter's strong arms went around her, pulling her against his chest. She stayed there until the vertigo passed and her legs gained enough feeling to hold her up.

"I hate him."

"I know, but you handled the conversation well."

"You mean because I didn't scream 'murderer' into the phone?"

"That and the fact that you arranged a meeting with him so that I can assess the situation and lay out the operation."

"Fine, as long as that's Operation Send Dane to Jail."

"It's Operation Send the Guilty to Jail."

"One and the same." Fatigue dropped over her like weights, but her mind showed no signs of shutting down. "Can we talk outside?"

"Sure. I'll meet you on the front porch in two minutes. I just need to make one quick stop in the kitchen first. And you might want to slip into something *less* comfortable."

Damn! She was standing there practically in Cutter's arms wearing nothing but a T-shirt that was too big and too short. She hadn't noticed how much of her was exposed until now. Apparently, Cutter had.

Even after the fact, it bothered her enough that she felt the burn in her cheeks. In spite of everything, there was no way to forget what they'd shared. The chemistry had simply been too hot to ever cool down completely. At least for her.

All in the past. The present was more than enough to deal with now. She rummaged in Merlee's closet for something to slip into as Cutter's footsteps receded down the hall.

She found a flowered caftan, a couple of sizes too big and in a shade of orange that made Linney's red hair look as if it were on fire. By contrast, her complexion paled to a washed-out tint of pink.

Gaudy, but decent, she padded to the porch in her bare feet and dropped to the wooden porch swing. The chains squeaked eerily as the night closed in around her and she felt herself sliding into the depths of gloom she'd faced when she'd first heard about Amy's drowning.

Cutter joined her, carrying two glasses filled with tinkling ice and an amber liquid. He handed her one. She put it to her lips and the odor overwhelmed her. "I don't drink whiskey."

"Think of it as medicine."

"I'm not sick."

"You're wound so tight you might shoot into orbit at any moment."

She took a sip and felt the burn travel down her throat and settle in her stomach. The anger and irritation welded into a seamless blue funk. "This is all a game to Dane, an unspeakably evil game."

"Why don't you start at the beginning and tell me everything he said?"

She nodded and took another sip of the whiskey. She still didn't like the taste, but the burn to her throat and nostrils seemed to clear her mind for the moment.

Cutter balanced himself on the porch banister and listened patiently until she'd covered everything. "I feel better that she's staying with Amy's mother. I think it may do her good to get out of the house."

"Were Amy and her mother close?"

"She didn't talk about her mother much, but I know she drove out to the Woodlands to visit her on occasion. I don't recall her ever saying that Dane went with her on those visits. Oh, and I know Edna took Amy and Julie to a local water park for Julie's third birthday."

"What about Amy's father? Is he around?"

"No. Her parents were divorced when she was a baby. They'd lost touch with him years ago. As far as I know, he wasn't even at Amy's funeral."

"That explains why he didn't go after Dane with a baseball bat when he battered his daughter. What about siblings?"

"She was an only child. Where are you going with this?"

"If Amy was afraid of Dane or if he'd ever made threats against her, there's a good chance she told someone—like her mother, or a sister if she had one. If a family member went to the GHPD, it might stir more action than your complaints generated."

"If Amy's mother has any suspicions of murder, she's hiding them well."

"What do you mean?"

"One of the local TV stations interviewed her and Dane the night of the drowning. She actually leaned on him at one point as if he were her pillar of strength. It turned my stomach."

"Do you know how to get in touch with her?"

"I know her name is Edna Sears and that she lives in the Woodlands. That's it."

"I think we should pay her a visit."

"Good idea. We can offer to take Julie to her house to pick up her things and then drop her off with Amy's mother."

"Sounds like a plan. The more immediate plan should be for you to go to bed and get some rest."

"The Navy made you bossy."

"I was always bossy. The Navy taught me to sound authoritative."

"Were you ever afraid, Cutter? I mean when you were thousands of miles from home, surrounded by the enemy with gunfire shattering the night?"

"Lots of times. A little fear can heighten your senses and help keep you alive. The trick is to never let it cloud your mind or dull your will. Like a woman, it can consume you if you let it."

He stood and took her hand, pulling her to her feet. "You don't have to be afraid, Linney. I'll keep you safe."

Her hand lingered in his. She was standing in his personal space, so near she could feel his breath on her skin. Her pulse quickened and the familiar memories flooded her mind. Heat darted through her, settling in places where she shouldn't feel anything tonight.

The impulse to stretch to her tiptoes and find his mouth with hers was all but overpowering. Just one quick taste to see if his lips still held the same salty-sweet flavor that had driven her wild in San Diego in what seemed like another lifetime.

He dropped her hand quickly, as if he'd been burned by the same sizzle that had gripped her. "Get some rest," he said, dismissing the sensual tension as if it were nothing. "You'll need it to deal with Dane."

And for dealing with Cutter and a desire that didn't have the decency to just fade away.

CUTTER WOKE AT DAYBREAK. He'd slept very little, but losing one night's sleep would have hardly any effect on his mental or physical functioning. He'd learned to deal with sleep deprivation and exhaustion in training and in the countless operations that followed.

He stretched and kicked back the sheets he'd spread on the sofa. There were plenty of empty beds in the house, but they were upstairs, too far away from Linney and Julie in case there had been trouble.

He reached for the gun beneath his pillow, a black-handled Smith & Wesson that he'd owned for years. There were also rifles and shotguns in the house. Firearms had been part of Cutter's life long before he'd gone into the military. Uncle Hank had seen to it that he not only learned to shoot but to handle all types of weapons with respect for the damage they could inflict.

Cutter's parents had died in a car accident on I-45 when he was two. Hank was his dad's brother and they'd run the ranch together. Hank and Merlee had raised Cutter from that point on.

He didn't remember his parents at all, though Merlee had talked about them when he was growing up and kept pictures of them around the house. He'd always thought he should miss them, or at least miss the idea of having parents. The truth was he hadn't. Merlee and Hank had filled the vacated positions too well. They'd never had children of their own.

He dropped to the hooked rug and started doing pushups, not counting them, just pushing his body to the limit. Only then did he get up and head for a cold shower. After that he'd go upstairs to his old room and see if he could find the leather shoulder holster he'd bought on one of his trips into Mexico when he'd still lived on the ranch.

He hadn't expected to start carrying a gun around Dobbin and Houston, but last night's attack on Linney made it a necessity for now. He had a permit that he'd applied for when he'd first returned to Dobbin. It had been easy to get with his experience and expertise, and he'd thought at first he might apply for a job in the security field.

Even if Dane *had* killed his wife, Cutter couldn't see him being stupid enough to try to kill Linney over unsubstantiated accusations. But stranger things had happened. He'd know more after he talked to the man himself. Cutter had an uncanny ability to read people. Knowing who not to trust had saved his own life a couple of times.

Too bad that same skill at reading people didn't work with Linney. It could have saved him a heartache that had been years in the healing. And still he couldn't look at her without aching to make love to her and start the whole damn process all over again.

DANE STIRRED FROM A DEEP SLEEP and reached for the piercing alarm, nearly knocking over the half glass of water on his bedside table. He punched the Off button, but the ring continued.

The phone. He finally opened his eyes enough to glance at the digital reading. Ten past seven. He muttered a string of curses under his breath. This had better be good, like a major break in last night's double homicide.

He grabbed the receiver and managed a groggy hello.

"Dane, it's Edna."

Amy's mother. He raked the hair off his forehead and pushed himself up on his elbows. "Morning."

"Did I wake you?"

"Yeah. I worked until the wee hours of the morning."

"I can't believe they made you go back to work so soon."

"The department is short-staffed. Summer vacations are in full swing and one of the women detectives is on maternity leave. I hated to say no."

"Then I'm really sorry I woke you, but I just wanted to clear everything with you."

"You're still picking up Julie at nine, aren't you?"

"There's been a slight change in plans. I got a call from Amy's friend…"

She choked on Amy's name. Edna was taking her death really hard. Maybe having her keep Julie wasn't that great an idea, but she'd begged him to let Julie visit for a few days.

"Who called you?" he asked, hoping she'd just get on with it.

"Linney Kingston."

That bitch. She was going to drive him right over the edge with her meddling and accusations. A pounding started between his temples. "What did she want?"

"To see how I was doing. She said she kept Julie for you last night. That was really thoughtful of her."

"Yeah. Real thoughtful."

"Linney offered to drop Julie off here after she stopped by your house to pick up her clothes and a few toys. I didn't want to impose on her but she said she was going to be in my area today anyway."

"That's convenient." He struggled to keep his tone level, then considered whether he should just come out and tell Edna that Linney thought he'd killed Amy before Linney told her. But officially, he wasn't supposed to know that.

He wouldn't if his partner hadn't overheard the conversation between her and one of the GHPD clerks. Probably best to keep playing ignorant of that fact for now.

"I told her to be sure and bring Julie's favorite teddy bear," Edna continued. "I know Julie doesn't sleep without it."

"I'll see that she brings it."

"I can keep Julie as long as you need me to, Dane. She's the only link I have now to—"

Sobs cut off the rest of her sentence. Dane blew out a quick breath. He couldn't deal with this. "I know you'll take good care of her, Edna. She needs a lot of love and attention right now."

"I promise I won't cry all the time. I'll get hold of myself for Julie."

"That would be good. I really have to go now."

"Take care of yourself, Dane. You were a good husband and Amy knew you loved her. Just try to focus on that."

"Yeah. I'll do that."

Fury pulsated through Dane like a jackhammer as he hung up the phone. How dare Linney call Edna and arrange to transport Julie and her things to the Sears household?

Edna Sears saw it as a favor. Dane saw it for what it was—a ploy to gain some tidbit of information to use against him. She was wasting her time. His alibi was airtight. But if she dug around in Amy's life too much she just might open a Pandora's box that no one could close. Edna knew that as well as he did.

JULIE STILL WASN'T TALKING or acting like the precocious, outgoing child she'd been before her mother's drowning, but she'd eaten a blueberry-topped waffle and drank a glass of orange juice, all compliments of Merlee's freezer.

Linney had helped her bathe after that and dressed her in the freshly laundered clothes from the day before. She'd laundered her own as well. Now she was trying to brush the tangles from Julie's long, curly locks.

"Sorry, sweetie, but this has to be done or your beautiful hair will look like a mess. And guess where you're going today."

Julie looked up, letting her gaze meet Linney's in the mirror for the briefest of seconds before yanking her head to the side again. Having her hair brushed was clearly not one of her favorite activities.

"Cutter and I are taking you to your grandmother's house. You're going to stay with her for a while. Won't that be nice?"

No reaction from Julie. Linney finished untangling Julie's hair and then pulled it back into a ponytail, using a band she'd found in a china bowl on Merlee's nightstand.

"First we'll stop off at your house so you can get some of your clothes and toys to take with you. You can pick which toys."

Still no reaction. "And you can see your daddy."

Julie pulled a lock of her hair into her mouth and stared at the floor. Linney dropped to her knees and pulled her into her arms. The girl felt so small and vulnerable that Linney had to fight the hot tears that burned at the back of her eyes.

So young and innocent and so much to cope with. She needed her mother, and Linney was a poor substitute for Amy. Images flashed in Linney's head. Mother and daughter swinging in the park the day the three of them had gone on a picnic. Julie serving her and Amy tea from the tea set Linney had given her for her birthday. Amy and Julie laughing and playing in the pool where Amy had drowned.

Oh, God. This hurt. Poor Julie. For her the mother/daughter memory making would come to a dead end so very early in her life.

"Daddy…"

Linney's heart slammed into her chest at the tremor in Julie's quiet whisper.

"Are you two ready to go?" Cutter asked from the bedroom door.

His timing couldn't have been worse. Linney silenced him with a look. "What about your daddy, Julie?"

Julie let her arms fall from Linney's neck. "Daddy hitted the bad man with his fists."

Chapter Five

Daddy hitted the bad man with his fists.

The words were still crawling around inside Cutter's head when he pulled into the driveway of the home that Dane Colley had shared with his wife and daughter until a few days ago.

The neighborhood was well-kept, on the southern side of Green's Harbor, a mile or so from the bay. The house was a brick, ranch-style structure Cutter would guess to be about twenty years old. The kind of house a detective and teacher's aide could easily afford.

Two huge pots of feathery ferns sat like sentinels at the door. Blooming Mexican heather bordered the covered porch, and some type of colorful annual spilled over from the flowerbeds.

Just your average American family in your average American suburb, Cutter thought, except that the wife had supposedly stumbled into the backyard pool and drowned.

It was a pretty sure bet that Dane had abused his wife. But had he killed her? Was he the man who wanted Linney dead or was someone else in the bizarre mix? Like the bad man whom Dane had hit with his fists.

Hopefully, Cutter would gain a better feel for Dane's guilt or innocence over the next half hour. In the meantime he'd called Goose and asked for a copy of the police report following the drowning.

Dane was still buttoning a light-blue sport shirt when he answered the door. The shirttail was out. His face was drawn, the muscles tight, and there was a small, unhealed scratch on his right cheek. No sign of a smile when he looked down at his daughter. No warmth in his steely-gray eyes.

"Good morning, pumpkin." Dane bent and reached out his arms to his daughter as if to pick her up. She held on to Linney's leg and he patted her on the head instead, tousling her hair as his gaze settled on Cutter.

"Who are you?"

Couldn't get more straightforward than that. "My name's Cutter Martin."

"He's a friend of mine," Linney said.

Dane stepped aside for them to come in, but there was no indication that he was glad to have them.

He stooped so that he was eye level with Julie and took her hands in his. "Daddy has to work on a big case so you're going to Grandma's for a few days. I have your suitcase all packed but you can go upstairs and pick out the toys you want to take with you."

Julie didn't say a word. She just stood perfectly still, sucking on a strand of her hair and peering at Dane from beneath her dark lashes.

"I'll go upstairs with her," Linney said.

Dane moved to block her exit. "No, we need to talk." He glared at Cutter. "Alone."

"Anything you have to say you can say in front of me," Cutter said.

"Fine." He turned his attention back to Linney. "Why did you call Amy's mother?"

"We're going right by there. I thought I'd do her a favor and drop Julie off. She seemed appreciative."

"Is that the only reason?"

"Of course. Why do you ask?"

The tendons in Dane's neck grew taut. "I just don't want you to say anything to Edna that would trouble her."

"She's already upset, Dane. She buried her daughter."

"Look, Linney, I know Amy talked to you the day before she died. She probably told you we'd been arguing. But it was nothing. I loved Amy and she loved me. I'd just rather Edna not know that we'd spent our last night arguing. If she gets upset, she'll upset Julie even more."

A yellow rubber ball came bouncing down the stairs. They all turned as the ball rolled across the floor until Dane stopped it with a stamp of his foot. Julie was standing at the top of the landing, saying nothing, but it was clear she'd been crying.

Dane took the steps two at a time and picked her up. "I'll help you get your toys. How about your Candyland game? You like to play that with Grandma? And the dolly Mommy got you from Toys "R" Us. You can take the doll's stroller, too. And I'll put your tricycle in the bed of the truck."

Linney walked to the built-in bookcase in the family room just off the kitchen and started perusing the framed snapshots that were scattered over the shelves, most of Julie, some of Julie with Dane and a person he assumed to be Amy.

Cutter followed.

"That's Amy," Linney said, pointing to one of the family photos. "She was beautiful, wasn't she?"

"Absolutely stunning." The woman looked like a model or a young starlet—a sylphlike brunette with full, pouty lips and beautiful eyes.

"And Dane's lying," she whispered, so low that Julie wouldn't hear. "He's not worried about Edna or Julie.

He just wants me to butt out of everything and let him get away with murder."

Linney was totally convinced of the man's guilt. Cutter still had his doubts, but he was a cautious man. Focus on one aspect of the danger and another would come up and bite you in the behind.

Cutter walked through the kitchen and to the back door for a glimpse of the pool. It was enclosed inside a six-foot-high chain-link fence. The gate appeared to be locked. The pool itself was rectangular, narrow with steps leading into what seemed no more than a wading pool before gradually growing deeper.

A slide dropped into the far end, and a blow-up ring with the head of a dinosaur floated on the surface. The self-propelled vacuum was making its rounds. It looked like a great place for a family to while away hot Texas afternoons.

Dane's voice carried from the kitchen. Apparently, he'd come back downstairs and was ready to load Julie's things into the truck. Cutter would love a chance to talk to him alone but doubted he'd get it.

His cell phone rang. It was Goose. Cutter stepped out the back door and took the call. "Did you get the report?"

"I did. Interesting situation, but it looks like an open-and-shut case. Husband came home and found his wife, said to be a good swimmer, fully dressed and facedown in the pool. He pulled her out and tried to revive her. When she didn't respond, he called an ambulance."

"What time of day was that?"

"One p.m. He said she'd complained of a headache that morning, so he'd stopped in to check on her. Apparently, she had a history of seizures."

Seizures. Cutter hadn't read that in the newspaper

account, nor had Linney mentioned it. It definitely cast a new light on things. "Was Dane by himself when he found her?"

"Yeah."

"Where was the daughter?"

"Inside the house, apparently watching a Disney movie. He claims he didn't know she was home until after the ambulance arrived and she wandered outside."

"Where was she supposed to be?"

"Day care. He said his wife took her on Tuesdays and Fridays in the summer so that she could be around other children."

"All that is in the police report?"

"It's pretty thorough."

"And there was no mention of anyone else being on the scene?"

"Nope. The report specifically states that Dane Colley was alone when he found the body. The officer who took the report said one of the lounges near the pool was turned on its side as if someone had tripped over it. The nozzle to the water hose was lying next to it and the water had been left on."

Which would fit with the scenario of Amy having had a seizure while watering the flowerpots around the pool. "So there was nothing to suggest foul play?"

"Not a thing, but I checked the autopsy report as well."

"Any evidence of a struggle there?"

"A mild blow to the head and bruises on one side of the face could have come from hitting the side of the pool upon falling."

"Any other bruises?"

"Old ones on the arms and stomach, but nothing recent. Now how about you tell me about Linney Kingston?"

Kingston. The name of Linney's ex-husband still

had the power to agitate Cutter. "She's just a friend. We both grew up in Dobbin, though she was a few years behind me in school." A few. Make that five. She was only thirteen when he'd been a senior in high school, far too young for him to have noticed her sexually until he'd run into her that long-ago September in San Diego.

"This old neighborhood chum wouldn't also happen to be a single hottie, would she?"

"You might say that."

"You go, buddy. But looks like she's all wet and sandy with her suspicions of foul play. I did a thorough check of all Colley's pertinent records. I don't see any red flags. No history of brutality or excessive force in the execution of his duties. No record of any domestic violence from the marriage."

"What about Amy's history?

"Bit of a problem there. I can't find anything on Amy until their marriage almost three and a half years ago."

"Three and a half?"

"Yep. Let's see… Here it is. It will be three and a half years exactly on June twenty-fourth."

And this was the seventeenth. Interesting, since Linney had mentioned Julie's third birthday. "Does the police report specifically state that Dane Colley is the biological father?"

"Hold on a sec and let me make sure." Goose made a buzzing noise while he scanned the report. "Yep, it says right here that Detective Colley is the biological father of Julie Colley and that the victim was the biological mother."

"Thanks, Goose. I owe you one."

"Naw. I'm still paying you back for those times you saved my butt. But if you're into police reports, Houston's always looking for good cops."

"You keep saying that, but I just don't think it's the

job for me, not after hearing you complain about the bureaucracy, the politics and the rules."

"You got a point there, but at least it keeps me on my toes. Ever wish you were back with the SEALs?"

"Every day, man." Every friggin' day of his life. But he had to admit that ever since Linney had appeared in his life, things had been anything but dull. "I have to run now, but we'll grab a beer and catch up on all this and more later."

"Book it. Just be careful, man. Texas isn't the badlands you're used to playing in. You can go to jail here for sticking your nose too far into someone else's business, especially if that someone is a police detective."

"I'll keep that in mind."

Cutter's immediate worry was keeping his testosterone in check once they dropped off Julie at her grandmother's and he and Linney were all alone.

"One more thing you should know before you get in this too deep, Cutter. You can't take this as gospel, but if it's accurate, it pretty much blows Linney's theory right out of the water."

"Hit me."

Cutter listened. Linney was not going to like what he heard.

LINNEY PULLED DOWN the visor mirror and checked her reflection as Cutter backed out of Dane's driveway. Her hair was a mess, the curse of not having the right products at the ranch. Fortunately, she'd all but given up makeup since divorcing Al, so the lipstick and blush she'd had in her purse had served her fine.

Al had liked her with layers of makeup and dressed to kill, especially when they'd gone to parties. Slinky designer dresses, four-and-a-half-inch Manolo Blahnik heels, neck, ears and fingers dripping with diamonds.

Trophy wives were meant to be seen and drooled over by envious men. Too bad she'd been too young and vulnerable to realize that that's what she was in for before the live production of the Houston wedding of the decade.

And now Al was in trouble with the Feds. She'd had little time to think of his current predicament since hearing about it on last night's news. Now that she did, she wondered if it would have any implications for her.

It shouldn't. The business was all in his name. The prenup made that crystal clear—or at least she'd thought it had before the division-of-assets provisions had become involved in complex, haranguing points by her attorney and Al's team of sharks.

She couldn't complain. She'd fared a lot better than Amy. Dane's loving husband act this morning hadn't changed Linney's mind about him one iota. She'd love to get Cutter's opinion on the murderous monster, but that would have to wait until they'd dropped off Julie.

She raked her fingers through her hair in a futile attempt to tame it. Not that neat hair would help her appearance all that much with remnants of the stain from the spaghetti-sauce incident still discoloring the most conspicuous spot on her shirt.

"I only live a few blocks from here," she said. "I'd like to stop by the house and change into something more presentable."

"Just tell me when to turn. You can pack a bag and a toothbrush while you're at it."

"Why?"

"So you won't have to wash your clothes every night at the ranch."

"I'm not—" She shifted and checked on Julie who was looking at a picture book she'd brought from her house. "I'm not a K-I-D-N-A-P-P-E-R anymore. I don't have to be on the run."

"Are you forgetting the highway S-N-I-P-E-R?"

"No, but I have an alarm system at my house. I'll be fine. I don't expect you to take me on full-time."

"I didn't offer full-time, just the immediate, fore-seeable future."

Of course that was all he'd offered. She turned to study the planes and angles of his profile as he slowed for a stop sign. She'd had a mad crush on him for half her life. Not that he'd ever noticed until that moonlit night she'd practically walked right into him on a stretch of warm California sand.

He'd asked her for a nightcap. The date had lasted five days. Fire crept inside her as the memories took over, running hot between her thighs and settling like simmering ashes in her core.

She imagined her hands on his chest, her fingers slipping between the fabric of his shirt and his flesh as she loosened the buttons, then—

"Tell me when."

"When?" Her cheeks burned.

"When do I turn to get to your house?"

She swallowed hard and tried to stamp out all the flames of desire that were still wreaking havoc with her voice and reflexes.

"One more block and then take a left on Redbud Drive. I'm the fourth house on the right. The reddish brick with the crepe myrtles in the front yard."

She turned and explained to her young charge that they were going to her house for a few minutes before they went to Julie's grandmother's.

The child looked like a lost, woebegone nymph. Linney's heart cratered, putting the situation into dismal, heartbreaking perspective and adding a layer of guilt to her conscience for the thoughts she'd had seconds before.

She rummaged in her handbag for her keys as Cutter stopped the car in her driveway. It dawned on her then that she'd left the garage-door opener in her car. "You get Julie, I'll unlock the door," she said. She had already pushed the door open by the time Cutter and Julie reached the covered portico.

Her stomach revolted at the sight, and hard shudders shook her until she had to hold on to the doorframe to keep from sinking to her knees.

"Take her back. Get Julie away from here," she said.

Cutter pushed past Linney. "Son of a bitch."

Linney turned and swooped Julie up in her arms, backing away before the child saw the horrors waiting just beyond the open door.

Chapter Six

Cutter stood in the doorway staring at the snapshots of Amy that had been blown up and plastered all over the walls of the foyer. All were of her in various states of undress, most portraying her in disgustingly lewd positions with a variety of men. All appeared to have been taken several years earlier when Amy was probably barely out of her teens.

A half dozen videos were haphazardly stacked on the entryway table, next to a vase of fragrant summer blossoms and silver-framed photographs. The top video was obviously porn, titled *Rich and Ready* and featuring "Ivana." Like the photos on the wall, the scantily clad woman on the video cover was a years-younger Amy Colley.

Cutter swallowed the curses that burned in the back of his throat. What kind of sick person would go to this kind of trouble to humiliate a dead woman? Not just a woman, the mother of a precious little girl. And why display the revolting pictures inside Linney's house?

There wasn't a doubt in his mind this was all connected to the attempt on Linney's life.

He took down the pictures, carefully touching only the taped edges in case they wound up as evidence in a trial. He stored them and the videos inside a lidded wicker basket that rested beneath the table. Getting them out of Julie's sight was the most important task now, but he'd take them to the Double M. They were all pieces to a villainous puzzle.

He checked the rest of the house room by room, thankful when there was no sign that the intruder had ventured past the foyer. Nothing at all amiss—until he reached Linney's bedroom.

One look past that door and shrapnel-strength anger penetrated every muscle. The sick bastard had raided Linney's lingerie drawer and chosen a black silk negligee and an assortment of lacy panties.

The negligee was draped suggestively across the bed. The panties were displayed at odd angles, one pair sliced up the front. The urge to kill swept through Cutter, as strong as it had ever been in the heat of battle.

He smashed his fist into the wall with such force it tore a ragged hole through the sheetrock. The echo of the crash rumbled around him, along with the answering clatter of Linney's sandals hurrying in his direction.

"Cutter, are you okay?"

"Yeah. Keep Julie back."

"She's in the kitchen."

But Linney was in the doorway, her face turning green.

"That rat," she muttered. "That dirty scumbag of a filthy rat."

The description fit. He just wished they had a viable suspect to go with it. The sordid display in the foyer didn't look like pictures a man would put up of his wife. But the lingerie strewn around the bedroom was clearly designed to frighten and intimidate Linney—to warn her off.

Torn between taking Linney in his arms or getting rid of the lewd exhibit, he chose the latter. He grabbed the clothing from the bed and balled it into a wad before tossing it to the floor inside her closet.

Linney yanked the coverlet and sheets from the bed as if they'd been contaminated. "Shows how much good going to the cops in Green's Harbor does, doesn't it? All my citizen's complaint against Dane did was make me a target."

Cutter couldn't argue the logic of that. It did settle one thing, though. "You're not staying in this house alone."

"I don't want to be in this house at all. Not now."

Good. He'd work better from the ranch and Linney would be safer there. His environment. The good guys playing on their home field, so to speak. His mind switched back to the more immediate.

"You said you have an alarm. Was it set?"

"No, I thought I was just running to pick up Julie when I left and that I'd be right back. This is a very safe area."

"I'll check for signs of a break-in."

"Why break in when all the intruder had to do was use the garage-door opener he could have easily stolen from my wrecked car before it was towed? The front and back doors to the house were locked, but not the one from the garage to the kitchen."

They could check that out with a call to the towing company. "Why don't you go ahead and change clothes," he said, "and pack what you'll need for a few days' stay in Dobbin. I'll check on Julie."

She nodded. "There's juice in the refrigerator and some cookies in a plastic bag in the pantry. Offer her both."

"I can handle that." He paused as he brushed past her. "Speaking of cookies, you're one tough one yourself."

"Thanks, cowboy."

He didn't mean to do anything then but clear out of her way, but her lips were right there. Inches from his. Maybe not exactly inviting but soft and seductive and— And he was just about to make a huge mistake. About to slip and set off an avalanche of emotions he might not be able to stop. He started walking.

"If you need me, I'll be in the kitchen."

"So THE INTERFERING BITCH didn't have the nerve to accuse you of murder to your face. That figures. She's not only a bleeding-heart troublemaker but a coward." Wesley Evans leaned his elbows on the Formica table-top that rested between them in the crowded booth and wiped a layer of grease from his hands.

"Yeah," Dane agreed, "and I think she's still bent on creating problems. No telling what Amy told her about me."

"It doesn't matter. Linney doesn't have a leg to stand on. The drowning was ruled an accident, and the chief knows you would never kill Amy. Hell, we all know that."

"Thanks for that vote of confidence."

"Have another onion ring," Wesley said, untangling one for himself from the nest of fried morsels. "Those hamburgers are taking forever."

Dane reached for an onion ring, popped it in his mouth and leaned back against the cracked plastic seat. This was the first time he'd had an appetite since the drowning. Getting out of the house and back to work had probably been the best thing for him.

"I didn't like the looks of the guy who tagged along with Linney."

"A boyfriend?" Wesley asked.

"Could have been, but he had an attitude, you know, like he might be cop or a private detective. He didn't say much but I had the feeling he was taking it all in, both of them just waiting for me to say the wrong thing or make the wrong move."

"You can check him out easily enough. What was his name?"

"Cutter Martin."

"That has a familiar ring to it."

"Yeah," Dane agreed. "I thought the same thing."

"How was Julie?"

"Lost without her mother. I'm not a lot of help. I've never been good with kids. Her grandmother dotes on her and Julie adores the woman. Edna will help her get past this better than I can."

"Yep. Kids recover quickly—except for my sixteen-year-old who's still angry at me for divorcing his mother. I hate to say it, bud, but you and Julie are probably both better off without Amy."

"Then don't say it."

"Okay, subject closed."

The waitress finally showed up with the burgers.

"Have to kill the cow?" Wesley asked.

"Funny. First time I've heard that line in at least ten minutes." She plopped the burgers on the table. The aromas of sautéed onion, sharp cheddar and jalapeños made Dane's mouth water. "Sarcastic servers," he said, "but still the best burgers in town."

"Sarcastic, but damn good-looking," Wesley said, watching as the shapely young waitress wiggled away.

"Stay away from her," Dane said. "She strips at Gordy's on the weekend. You can take 'em off the pole but you can't make them learn to settle for the two-step."

"You should know." Wesley bit into his burger, squirting mayonnaise and hot mustard from between the seeded bun.

Conversation stopped. Timing couldn't have been better. Wesley was an insensitive ass at times, but he was a super homicide man and they had a killer to catch. The home invasion was high profile, and the chief, as usual, wanted the case solved yesterday.

THE SLEEK BLACK PORSCHE pulled up in the driveway and stopped behind Cutter's truck just as Linney was locking the front door. The last thing she needed after the morning she'd had was a face-to-face encounter with her ex-husband, especially with him facing charges from the IRS this afternoon.

The truth was that in all the commotion since she'd heard last night's news, she's forgotten all about his troubles. But *his troubles* was the quintessential phrase here. She was not about to let him draw her into it.

Al got of his car, adjusted his designer sunglasses and then propped his personal trainer–firm buns against the front fender of his car, waiting for her to come to him. Cutter beat her to it.

"Are you looking for someone?"

"My wife."

"Your *ex*-wife," Linney corrected as she reached Cutter's side. "Did you forget our agreement? We talk only through our respective attorneys."

"I thought you might cut me some slack since I'm in a bit of a legal hassle with the Feds." He sneered in Cutter's direction. "Who's he?"

"A friend of mine."

"Cutter Martin," Cutter offered, extending a hand though Al hadn't.

"Oh, yeah, the Dobbin war hero. I read about you in the newspaper. Now if you'll excuse us, Cutter, Linney and I need to talk."

"I must have misunderstood," Cutter said. "I thought I just heard Linney say her lawyer would do any necessary talking."

"Exactly," Linney agreed. "Now if you'll excuse us, Al, we have a child waiting and it's hot out here."

"This will only take a minute."

Linney stared at her watch. "Okay. One minute, and the seconds are ticking away."

Finally, he took off his glasses and gave her a look that she assumed was designed to make her feel bad for him. It didn't work. For one thing he couldn't escape the egotistical vibes he put off. For another, she knew him too well.

"It's in both our best interests to settle the dissolution-of-property issues before I get caught up in a lawsuit with the Treasury Department."

"Fine. Let's settle. You have my offer—a line-by-line agreement with our prenuptial contract."

"That's not reasonable and you know it. Extenuating circumstances—"

"Your minute's up." Linney turned and walked toward the truck.

Al didn't budge.

"A minute's a little harsh," Cutter said. "I'll give you all of sixty-five seconds to get that little car out of my way. But not a second more. You know how we Dobbin war heroes are. We love demolition almost as much as we love good old-fashioned hand-to-hand combat."

"I'm not afraid of you, Mr. Martin."

Nonetheless, the Porsche was out of their way with thirty seconds to spare.

"Nice guy," Cutter said, as Al sped out of sight.

"He has his moments. They're just few and far between these days."

"I can't wait to hear the whole story."

"It's the typical one—Lies and Deceptions in the Lives of the Rich and Infamous. I'll fill you in later, after we've dropped Julie at her grandmother's."

"About that," Cutter said. "How about we stop at that park we passed on the way into your subdivision?

A lot's happened since we left the ranch this morning, and we need to talk before we see Edna Sears."

"If you're talking about those pictures that were plastered all over my walls, they were fake. Anyone with a computer and the right software program can doctor photos these days."

"It's not just that. I talked to Goose while you were getting Julie's toys together."

"Nothing you can say will convince me I'm wrong about what happened."

"No, but it might throw in an element of doubt."

LINNEY FIT HER HANDS on the smooth plastic swing seat and gave Julie a few firm pushes. Ordinarily, Julie would have screamed with delight and shaken her short legs at the excitement of it all. Today she didn't even manage a smile.

Reluctantly, Linney left her to swing on her own and joined Cutter on a nearby park bench. The swings and the bench were shaded by the leafy branches of huge oak trees that predated the park and subdivision by many decades.

A slight breeze whispered through the branches. Neither the shade nor the breeze would be enough to make the temperature tolerable by midafternoon, but right now it was almost pleasant.

Too bad the rest of her life wasn't in that same mode. "What is it I need to hear?" she asked, eager to get the bad news over with. She was sure it was bad news. It was the only kind she'd been getting lately.

"Did you know that Amy had a history of seizures?"

"No. She never mentioned it. Did Goose tell you that?"

Cutter nodded.

"How would he have found that out?"

"Dane mentioned it to the officer who did the cursory investigation of the drowning."

"That sounds exactly like some excuse he'd invent to explain why Amy might just fall into the pool and drown when she's an excellent swimmer. I'm not buying it."

Cutter slapped at a horsefly that lit on his arm. "Uncontrolled seizures might also explain bruises from time to time."

"I worked with Amy every day, Cutter. She never mentioned seizures and definitely never had one at the school. It's a crock, and Dane would have no reason for making up those lies if he was innocent."

"Amy's medical history will be easy enough to check."

"Or I can just ask her mother. I'm sure Edna will know."

Linney stood to go and give Julie another push, but Julie dropped from the swing on her own and went to the elaborate climbing, slide and tunnel structure. That could occupy her for hours, but Linney had no intention of being here that long. She leaned against the gnarly trunk of the oak nearest the bench, staying where she could keep an eye on Julie.

"What else did Dane lie about, or is that it?"

"Goose did bring up another issue."

And she knew from Cutter's expression that she wouldn't like this one, either. "What?"

"The police report taken at the scene indicated that Dane had spent the morning of the drowning teaching a class of new recruits about the procedures to follow when they were first on the scene at a homicide. The class lasted from eight-thirty to noon."

"He didn't report her dead until after one. If the class let out at noon, that still left plenty of time to kill her."

"The medical examiner placed the time of death at approximately ten o'clock."

Giving Dane the perfect alibi. Her irritation level climbed. "I told you Dane knows how to play the system. He killed Amy. I don't know how, and I don't know when, but it is just too coincidental to believe she just happened to drown on the same day she was planning to leave her physically abusive and controlling husband."

"It sounds that way, but—"

Linney's hand flew to her hip. "But nothing. He did it. Maybe he snuck away from the class just long enough to drive home and back. Maybe he's in league with the medical examiner, or the examiner may have just made a mistake."

"Whoa, there, sweetheart. Don't go firing blanks at the messenger. I'm just telling you what Goose found out."

"That's not the way it sounds."

Cutter was buying into Dane's game, the same way everyone else had. "You can back out of this at any time, Cutter. If you're convinced there's no crime, just drop me off at the car-rental agency and I'll pick up a vehicle and take Julie to Edna's by myself."

Cutter stood and covered the short distance between them in a couple of heartbeats. He wrapped his hands around her forearms, clutching her so tightly she felt his fingers digging into her flesh.

"I'm not going anywhere without you, Linney." His voice was low, but edgy. "But I work my way. No jumping to conclusions or ruling out possibilities. I don't know if Dane killed Amy. I do know that someone tried to kill you last night, and that's reason enough for me to stick around."

"This isn't about me."

"It is in my book. So tell me about Al Kingston. Why isn't he willing to abide by the prenuptial contract?"

"Al had nothing to do with the attempt on my life."

"The prenup," he insisted.

"Okay, for what it's worth, the contract specified that I receive 5 percent of the company's profit for each year of my marriage. At that time, the company was showing a profit of approximately two million dollars a year. By the last year we were married, those profits had risen to just under fifty million dollars a year, thanks to some major commercial contracts to furnish five-star hotels across the Middle East and several Saudi palaces."

"So he's decided that your share is too much?"

"His attorneys are arguing that the prenuptial agreement was made in good faith but that the business itself has changed from a Houston-based furniture chain to an international design and furnishing operation, and therefore the contract with me does not apply."

"I'm guessing he wants you to settle for a lot less."

"Four million dollars less, approximately half of the agreed-on settlement. I'm not giving it up without a fight." Al had enough cars, houses and vacation homes. She could put the money to much better use.

"Men have been known to kill for a lot less than four million, Linney."

"Al's not a killer. A liar and most likely a thief, as far as the IRS is concerned, but not a killer. He has attorneys to do his dirty work for him. They accomplish just as much with their legal shenanigans as psychos do with guns."

She was sure Al hadn't been behind the ambush last night, but she could see the doubt written all over Cutter's face. "You may know the military's type of war, Cutter. I know Al's. He's arrogant, greedy and immoral—but not murderous."

A crunching of pebbles caught Linney's attention. She looked toward the bike path that meandered through the trees at the edge of the playground. A man on a racing bike slowed almost to a stop, his gaze directed at Julie, who was perched on top of the wooden deck and noisily kicking the heels of her sneakers against one of the bars.

Apprehension crawled up Linney's spine. It was probably unwarranted, brought on by the events of the last few days, but the uneasy feeling spurred her to action. "Time to go, Julie," she called, walking toward her.

The man smiled and called to someone behind him. A few seconds later, two young boys on bikes joined him.

"Can we stop and play, Daddy?" one of the boys asked.

"For ten minutes. Then we have to go pick up your sister from swim class."

Okay, so her nerves were a wreck. It was still time to go. She had some questions for Edna Sears that needed answers. She'd make sure she had a chance to talk to her without Julie present, and she'd put her cards on the table.

Edna might not have known Amy was about to leave Dane, but she must have noticed the bruises Amy sported on a regular basis. And she'd know if Amy was prone to seizures.

Edna was Amy's blood kin. If she went to the GHPD with suspicions about Dane, they'd have to follow up on them. And as far as Dane's alibi was concerned, Linney was certain that would fall apart faster than a paper chain in a kindergarten game of tug-of-war.

EDNA PARTED THE DRAPES at the front window and peered through the open slat in the blinds. Her heart twisted at the sight of her precious granddaughter, who'd never see her mother again.

Amy had loved her daughter so much. Julie's birth had been as instrumental as Dane had been in helping Amy get her life together.

Edna understood all too well that the bond between mother and daughter was one of the closest on earth. It endured heartbreak and rejection and remained resilient enough to offer unconditional love. At least it had been that way for her.

Amy had been the very air Edna breathed from the day she'd come screaming into the world and the harried doctor had placed her in Edna's arms. Unmarried, unprepared and basically shut off from the world she'd known as a carefree teenager, Edna had attempted to be a good mother, but had probably fallen far short of the ideal.

Motherhood hadn't been her choosing. Her mistake had been deciding to walk home alone that long-ago night after choir practice.

The man had stopped to ask directions. Too late Edna had seen the knife and the wild gleam in his eyes. A sharp pain stabbed at Edna's chest, old and familiar but barely noticeable next to the new heartbreak.

She closed her eyes and forced herself back to the present. Julie was doing her funny little half skip up the walk. So young. So innocent. So precious.

That's why Edna absolutely could not let Linnette Kingston turn Amy's drowning into a media-fueled murder investigation. Amy hadn't deserved to die, but she did deserve to rest in peace. Most of all, Julie deserved to hold on to untarnished memories of the mother who'd loved her with all her heart.

The doorbell rang. Edna rushed to pull Julie into her arms. Amy's daughter was all she had left. Linney had to be stopped—no matter what it took.

Chapter Seven

Cutter watched with relief as Julie bounded into her grandmother's arms. The child was more animated than he'd ever seen her in the short time they'd been together. Edna held the girl close, the slightest of smiles crinkling the skin around her tormented eyes. He suspected that their time together would be good for both of them.

He knew what the trauma of death could do to individuals. He'd seen a frogman he'd thought was made of iron snap one hot day on the banks of a muddy river. The SEAL had seen the worst of war and even watched a buddy on his team get blown to bits. Yet it had been four words from the operator onboard the boat that had sent him over the edge.

Your son was killed.

With war raging all around him, it had been a head-on vehicular collision back in the States that had taken the heart right out of the man.

"Can I have a juice box?" Julie asked as she disentangled herself from her grandmother.

"Yes, but just juice," Edna said. "It's too close to lunchtime for a cookie."

"Yes, ma'am."

"Thanks so much for dropping my granddaughter

off," Edna said, as the child headed for the kitchen. "I would have driven to Green's Harbor to pick her up, but I dreaded the thought of going back to that house so soon after— Well, you know."

"I understand." Linney gave her a warm hug. "I'm glad we could help and it wasn't even out of our way."

"I thought you lived near Amy."

"I do, but Cutter doesn't."

Edna turned her attention to him. "You'll have to excuse me. I'm not thinking too clearly these days. You look familiar, but I can't place you. Did you also work with Amy at the kindergarten?"

"No, ma'am. I'm Cutter Martin, a friend of Linney's. I didn't know your daughter." He extended his hand and she slipped her much frailer one inside his. He'd guess her age at no more than fifty, if that old.

But she was bone-thin with graying hair, frizzy bangs in front but cut razor-short from her ears to the back of her head. Deep wrinkles cut into the flesh around her eyes and mouth. The years hadn't treated her kindly.

"Grandma, may I go to my room and play with my dollhouse?"

"Of course you can, sweetheart."

"I've fixed up the guestroom for her," Edna explained as Julie slurped from her juice box and walked away. "She's the only overnight company I ever have anyway, and it makes her feel at home when she comes over to stay with me."

"It's good that you have such a loving relationship," Linney said. "She'll need you even more now. She's barely talked at all since they called me from day care and told me she was crying hysterically."

"I'm glad they were able to get you. Dane was on that horrible case where two people were murdered inside their own home. He'll find the men responsible. He's one of the best detectives they have, but still it's a shame you can't even be safe behind your own four walls."

Definitely no indication that she thought of her son-in-law as a murderer, Cutter decided.

Edna motioned toward the sofa. "Would you like to sit down? I have a fresh pitcher of iced tea or I can make coffee."

"Nothing for me," Linney said.

"I could use a glass of tea," Cutter said. Actually, it did sound good. It was one of the things he'd really missed in the service. Good Texas tea, sweet and icy cold. There were nights he'd have taken it over a woman. Of course, Linney hadn't been around then.

He took a seat on the sofa. Linney walked over and stood behind him, leaning close to whisper in his ear.

"She may be close to Julie, but she was obviously not close to Amy. Had she been she would have known Dane is not the saint she seems to think he is."

"It could be an act on her part," Cutter said, "an attempt not to air dirty laundry in public." However, he had to admit it didn't look or sound like an act.

Linney walked over to one of the two built-in bookcases that flanked the fireplace and picked up a framed photograph of Amy.

"That one's my favorite," Edna said, returning with the tea and stopping for a second at Linney's elbow before handing him the glass and a coaster to catch the dripping condensation.

"That was her fifteenth birthday and I'd taken her and two of her friends to Galveston to celebrate. She was only five in this one," Edna said, picking up a photograph of Amy in a tutu.

Cutter didn't join them at the bookcase, but he could see enough of the grouped photos to know that they skipped at least a decade of Amy's life. There were no snapshots of her that appeared to be much past the fifteenth birthday party until the photo of a pregnant Amy.

Linney picked another photo. "This is a great picture of Amy."

"Yes," Edna agreed. "It was taken just days before Julie was born. Amy was convinced her stomach would never return to a normal size, but she lost the weight from the pregnancy in a matter of months.

"Amy hated this one, but I love it," Edna said, pointing to an eight-by-ten black and white of Amy and Dane. His left arm was around her shoulders, his right hand cradling her extended belly. They were both dressed in white shorts and T-shirts. Amy's shirt didn't quite close the gap between it and the waistband of her shorts.

Edna talked about the pictures until her voice got shaky and tears moistened her eyes. "I miss my Amy," she said. "I miss her so much."

"I miss her, too," Linney said. "Not the way you do, I know, but your daughter and I had grown really close."

"I'm glad. She needed a friend. Amy always needed her friends, even with Dane and Julie claiming so much of her time. She was such a special person. And it's all lost now. Just gone. She'll never be back."

Edna pulled a tissue from her pocket and dabbed at her wet eyes.

Tears glistened in Linney's eyes as well, but Cutter could still read the determination in every line of her face. She turned away from the photographs and put a hand on Edna's arm. "Did you ever think the drowning might not have been an accident?"

Edna's back stiffened and she jerked her arm away. "Of course not. What are you suggesting?"

"Just that I hung out with her and Julie at the pool a few times. She was an excellent swimmer. When I asked her about it, she said that her high-school swim team won the state competition when she was a freshman."

"They did, and Amy was one of the best on the team, but Dane and the officer who answered his emergency call said that she tripped and fell into the water. They concluded that she must have had a seizure and passed out."

"Amy never mentioned having seizures, and I never knew her to have a problem like that when we were teaching together."

"She wouldn't have said anything about her tendency to lose consciousness for fear that the school board wouldn't hire her. She loved her work. And you're right. It didn't interfere with her job performance."

"Then she did have a history of seizures?"

Edna looked away, casting her eyes toward the tips of her white sandals. "Yes."

She was lying. Cutter was as certain of that as he was of his own name. He'd spotted fake informants in the military with an accuracy record that put the best lie detector to shame.

But why lie to protect someone who might have killed her daughter?

"Did you ever question Amy about her bruises?" he asked, stepping over to stand beside her and Linney.

Not only did Edna continue to avoid eye contact, but she shifted nervously, cramming her hands into the deep pockets of her full cotton skirt. "What bruises?"

The question seemed legitimate. It was possible Amy had avoided her mother after Dane had hit her. It would make sense that she wouldn't want to upset her.

"She frequently came to work with bruises," Linney said.

"I don't doubt that," Edna said. "Amy bruised easily. Once she bumped her hip against my kitchen table and it looked as if she'd fallen from a five-story building.

She had bruises from time to time, but nothing she couldn't easily explain."

"Then you never suspected that Dane was abusing her?" Linney asked.

"Most definitely not. Dane adored her from the day he met her. She could get away with anything with him. Besides, Amy would have never taken abuse off him or anyone else. She stood up for herself."

"Maybe not," Linney said, her voice softening. "I had coffee with Amy the afternoon before she drowned. She told me she was leaving Dane, that she couldn't take his control and abuse any longer."

Edna started to shake and her face turned a ghostly white. "I don't believe you," she said, no longer looking away, but staring at Linney as if she were some horrid phantom who'd come to torment her. "Why would you come here and say such things?"

"Because they're true. I'm sorry to upset you, Mrs. Sears. Really sorry, but Amy was leaving Dane that very day and I think he may have killed her to keep her from doing that."

"No. No." Edna backed away. "If she told you that, they must have had an argument. Amy may have been angry but she wouldn't have left. She loved Dane. He loved her."

"Perhaps she just didn't want to hurt you by telling you the whole truth about their marriage," Cutter offered.

Edna covered her face with her hands. "I want you to go now," she said. "I need you to go and stop trying to spread ugly rumors about my daughter."

"I don't want to hurt Amy's memory," Linney insisted. "I'm trying to get justice for her. I've been to the GHPD with my suspicions. They blew me off. I also went to the local news media. They said they couldn't look into unfounded suspicions when a respected law enforcer's reputation was at stake."

"Then why come to me with these horrible suggestions?"

"You're Amy's mother. The police would have to take complaints from you seriously. Please, go to them and ask for an investigation. What can it hurt?"

Edna shook her head. "Just leave, Linney. Please, just stop making these insane accusations before you do some real harm."

"Okay, but think about it. For Amy's sake."

"Please, just go."

Linney shrugged. "Is it okay if I say goodbye to Julie first?"

Edna only managed a nod. She watched Linney walk away and go to the kitchen. Cutter followed her.

"Amy didn't have epilepsy, did she?"

Edna pressed the balls of her hands against her temples and closed her eyes. When she finally opened them, she curled her fingers around the top of a straight-backed kitchen chair. "Why are you doing this to me?"

"I'm just trying to help. Did Amy have seizures?"

Edna made a guttural cry, as if she were experiencing a pain deep inside her chest. Finally, she met Cutter's gaze. Her eyes had a haunted look he'd seen in dying men fighting for a last breath.

"No," she murmured, "at least not what most people think of as seizures. Amy dabbled in drugs when she was younger. You know how kids are when they get with the wrong crowd."

"What kind of drugs?"

"Crack. Acid. Whatever she could get her hands on. Anyway, she still had problems from that sometimes. Not often anymore, but occasionally."

"Problems? Like hallucinations?"

"Yes. When they hit, she'd get disoriented and then she'd just black out. It happened several times when she was pregnant but only once since Julie was born. And she always had warning signs before they hit—usually a severe headache and nausea. It gave her time to call for help or to stop driving if she was in a car."

"Did she call for help Friday morning?"

"No, and that's the really puzzling thing. But you can see why I don't want her past drug problems to leak to the news media. It wouldn't help and someone might make negative comments about Amy to Julie."

"Is that why you lied to Linney?"

"Yes. I don't want her taking that information back to the kindergarten center. I don't want to see Amy's memory tainted by things so far in her past. I'm only telling you now because I can see you aren't going to stop asking questions until I level with you."

"Linney doesn't want to hurt Amy or Julie. You need to realize that."

"I do, and I know who you are now. I realized it while I was getting our tea. You're that Navy SEAL guy who was in the newspaper and on TV. You were shot in some kind of ambush, but they gave you a medal for bravery."

"None of that has anything to do with my being with Linney today."

"But you're a hero. Be one in this by just letting my daughter's tarnished past stay in the past. Convince Linney to stop meddling in what doesn't concern her."

He'd love to, if it were as easy as that. But Linney was in this up to her gorgeous green eyes, and things had already moved past the danger mark.

He walked over and wrote his cell number down on a scratch pad near the kitchen phone. "Think about what Linney told you and call me if you want to talk. Day or night."

"I won't call."

But Cutter was almost certain that she would after

she had had a chance to think about what Linney had told her. A woman who loved her daughter couldn't ignore facts indicating that her daughter might have been murdered. Nor would she stand by and let the man responsible simply walk away from the crime.

In the meantime, he had Linney to keep safe and himself to keep from crossing the line with Linney. Making love with her would no doubt be as earth-stopping and skyrocketing as it had been six years ago.

It would also throw him right back into the same situation as before. She hadn't been willing to settle for a cowboy warrior six years ago and there was no reason to think she'd feel differently now. She was fighting too hard for her $8 million settlement.

A man who wouldn't be defeated couldn't be defeated.

A great adage that had served him well in battle. It had flown out the window the second Linney had appeared on the scene.

LINNEY MONOPOLIZED THE DISCUSSION as they drove away, venting her frustration with Edna Sears. Cutter was still tossing the situation about in his mind like dice on a roulette table. Ten minutes of that and his stomach finally said enough.

They stopped at a restaurant that Linney suggested, an English pub that sat on the banks of a narrow ribbon of water that meandered from the Woodlands Mall to an outdoor pavilion and beyond.

The restaurant overlooked the water and a row of bal-conied, luxury condominiums. It had the ambience of the San Antonio Riverwalk, minus the history.

"How did you find this place?" he asked.

"I discovered it when I came out to the pavilion with some of the other teachers for a Harry Connick Jr. concert. Now, that is one sexy man."

"Sexier than I am?" he teased.

"No one is sexier than you, Cutter Martin."

"Guess that means you expect me to buy."

"Well, of course. Do you mind if we sit outside? I know it's warm but there's cloud cover and they have fans."

He glanced at the sky as they took the outside steps down to the patio seating. He'd been so preoccupied with his thoughts that he hadn't noticed the clouds that had rolled in. There were darker clouds off to the north indicating that afternoon thundershowers were a real possibility.

"Outside's fine." He chose a seat where his back would be against the wall and he had a good view of everyone who came and went. He didn't expect trouble out in the open like this, but he hadn't expected to see a machine gun jutting from the window of that car last night, either. Underestimating the enemy could lead to major mistakes.

There were a dozen tables outside, about half of them occupied, many with young mothers lunching with children. Two preschool boys were playing with tiny metal cars on the walk just beyond the serving area. One table overflowed with teenage girls who were giggling and dipping their spoons into a single dish of a whipped cream–topped chocolate dessert.

"Will you have a glass of wine with me?" Linney asked, appearing more relaxed now that they were surrounded by people not related to Amy Colley.

"I'm a beer man."

"Then I'll have a beer with you. On second thought, the margarita that lady's having looks good." She nodded her head in the direction of a young woman sitting nearby in a pair of shorts that barely skimmed her bottom and a halter top that covered just the essentials.

He grinned. "Looks good."

"I'm talking about the drink."

"So was I."

"Liar."

He exhaled slowly, amazed at how Linney incited a sexual energy in him without even trying. Odd the way he felt so much more alive with her in the picture.

The days since his injury and honorable discharge had gone by in a blur before she'd shown up, like living in a world of gray on gray. Now his senses crackled with awareness and his brain was absorbing details like a sponge.

Partly it was the fact that she turned him on. But the situation had revived his as well. Protecting Linney had become the major drive in his life. But there was also the conflicting evidence to sort out and the need to plan and carry out a viable operation.

Bottom line: He was doing something that mattered again.

The waitress took their drink orders and left them with menus. He opened his and scanned the offerings. Linney pushed hers to the side. "What was it like being a SEAL, Cutter?"

She seemed to have an uncanny ability to read his mind. "Which day?"

"Any day. Pick one."

"Some days were routine. Others were like walking a tightrope with no net and a firing squad to greet you if you made a wrong step."

"And yet you miss it?"

"Yeah. Call me crazy."

"No. I envy you. You're only five years older than I am, yet you've done remarkable things. You've saved lives. You've served your country. You know who you are."

"You haven't exactly been napping in clover. You've been married and divorced. Now you're a teacher."

"I fell into all of that with little effort."

"Hard to fall into a marriage, wasn't it?"

"Not when you're nineteen. Al was rich, sophisticated and charming. There was no real reason not to marry him."

"You didn't mention love."

"I convinced myself I was in love at the time."

"You didn't fall into a teaching degree."

"Almost. I was at A&M on a special program where if I taught for two years after graduation I didn't have to pay back the loan. I'd just finished my second year when I met Al."

No doubt the same summer he'd run into her. She'd fallen then, too. Fallen into the bed in his motel room. After five days and nights of sending Cutter to the moon with their lovemaking, she'd walked out without so much as a good-bye kiss.

Ancient history, he reminded himself. And this time history was not going to be repeated. "So when did you finish your degree?"

Linney turned to watch the waitress unload an overflowing tray of food at the table next to them, then leaned in and rested her elbows on their own empty table. She shrugged. "Are you sure you want to be bored by all this?"

"Go ahead. Bore my socks off. You got married and dropped out of school. So how'd you get the degree? Or did Al find a way to buy it?"

"No, but he paid off my loans, which is all I wanted at the time. I forgot all about school and a career until I realized my marriage was racing downhill at the speed of an Olympic toboggan. That's when I enrolled in the University of Houston and got my degree. I like kids, so I figured why not teach."

"That makes sense. And you still have plenty of time to have a houseful of your own kids."

"I hope to. Al wanted to put off having a family. In retrospect, I'm glad we did." Linney picked up the menu, looked at it for a second and was ready to order when the waitress arrived with their drinks. She opted for a grilled chicken salad. He went with the fish and chips.

Linney stirred her drink, then sipped slowly, letting the liquid flow over the layer of grainy salt that rimmed the edge. Her lips glistened with moisture when she set the glass back on the table. He imagined the taste of them and had to take a deep breath to keep the unwelcome rush of urges under control.

The muscles in his left leg started to knot up. He shifted so that he wouldn't kick her under the table when he stretched it out.

"Does your leg still give you pain?" she asked.

"Some, but it's getting better all the time."

"Does it hinder what you can do? I mean, other than the slight limp?"

So she'd noticed. He liked to think people didn't. He definitely didn't want pity from Linney. "I won't be running any marathons, but I'll be able to do almost everything else in time. I'm luckier than a lot of guys who took direct fire, so I'm not complaining."

"And you have a beautiful ranch to come back to." She took another sip of the margarita. "So why are you staying in Merlee's condo in town?"

Good question, but one he didn't exactly have the answer to. "I'm not quite ready to settle down on the ranch."

"Still have a wild streak, do you?"

He did and he was feeling it now in lots of places he'd just as soon would lie down and play dead. He wondered if Linney still had her wild streak.

And here he went again, right back to those five days and nights in San Diego when they'd made love for hours on end and found a million ways to please each other. There had been no hesitation, no embarrassment. No holding back. Just wild, wanton abandonment at its spectacular best. A meeting of needs and hunger and passion so intense he'd never imagined it could end.

A smarter, more experienced man would have known that nothing that hot wouldn't cool down. Songs had been written about that.

And now he'd take her back to the ranch with him and find some way to keep his sexual desires tamped down to just a slow burn instead of a roaring fire. He'd keep Linney safe if it was the last thing he ever did. But he'd be damned if he'd throw his heart onto the slaughterhouse floor again.

Thankfully, the food came and he dug into it as if he were ravenous. Food was a poor substitute for the thing he really craved, but at least it kept his hands and his mouth occupied.

Resisting her at the ranch house, with its comfortable crannies and seductive privacy, would prove more difficult, especially without Julie there to serve as a youthful chaperone. But he was hardened, battle-toughened. He'd make it through the days just fine.

The nights would be pure hell.

Chapter Eight

By four-thirty that afternoon, Linney was alternating between pacing the floor and staring out the huge family-room windows at the acres of pastureland and scattered trees that stretched behind the ranch house. Cutter had been busy or else deliberately ignoring her ever since they'd returned to the Double M.

He'd spent most of the time in the small study off the kitchen, either at Merlee's computer or on his cell phone. He claimed he was tracking down information on Dane Colley and her ex-husband. She suspected that he was checking out Amy as well.

There was no doubt plenty of information floating around the Internet about Alfred Russell Kingston. He'd been born into the Houston business world, so to speak.

Al had gotten his money the old-fashioned way. He'd inherited it. But he'd been the one to expand the business into the international marketplace.

Al's greed and ambition were renowned. He'd do anything short of auctioning off his own mother to make a profit. Tax fraud? Most likely. Spend a fortune on attorney fees to keep from paying her what the prenuptial called for? In a heartbeat.

Attempted murder? Not his style. Cutter was wasting

his time investigating Al. She'd tried to tell him that. He'd totally discounted her opinion.

But at least Cutter was doing something constructive. She envied him the tasks, especially since she had no idea how to go about proving that Dane had killed Amy. In her mind, going to the police with her suspicions should have been enough.

What she needed was for the drowning to draw the attention of one of the cable news channels. Once they got their teeth into a story, they gnawed it to the bone.

Linney went to the refrigerator for one of the diet colas she'd picked up at the supermarket in Magnolia. She popped open the can and took a long sip.

"I think we're on our way," Cutter said, waving a computer printout as he joined her in the kitchen.

"Good. On our way where?"

"To finding out about both Amy's and Dane's pasts. I called a private investigator Goose recommended. He's supposed to be one of the best in the area at uncovering well-hidden secrets."

"I'm not interested in Amy's past. Nothing she could have done was deserving of being killed."

"No, but it's hard to plan an operation with predictable outcomes if you're working with excessive unknown factors."

"Just concentrate on Dane. How sick can that man be to plaster the walls of my foyer with those disgusting fake pictures of Amy? Not to mention trying to kill me with his own daughter in the car."

"We don't have proof he did either of those at this point. But whoever did it is not only sick but probably desperate." Cutter raked his fingers through his hair, shoving it straight back. "I need some air," he said. "Are you up for taking a couple of the horses out for a ride?"

"Am I ever."

"I'll have Aurelio bring up the mounts from whatever pasture he has them in today."

"Perfect. I'll change into my tennis shoes and slather on sunscreen. I could use a hat. Do you think Merlee would mind if I wore one of hers?"

"Absolutely not, but we should buy you a Western hat. And some boots. Can't be a real cowgirl without the right duds."

"Yee-haw." Not that she was a cowgirl or had ever lived on a ranch. She was pretty sure, though, that a ranch needed a man like Cutter to make it exciting. She wasn't sure what men like Cutter needed. It obviously wasn't her. He knew she was single, but he'd made no attempt to re-create what they'd had in San Diego.

Not that she'd expected him to. Not that she needed or wanted another wham, bam, thank you, ma'am fling with no mention of love or affection.

Cutter disappeared down the hallway and she went to get ready for the ride. It wouldn't lessen her frustration, but a good horse beneath her, wind in her face and the heroic Cutter Martin at her side certainly couldn't hurt.

THE HORSES AURELIO had brought them were splendid. Linney's was Lacy Lu, a black beauty with a white snip on its nose and four white socks. Aurelio had said she was Merlee's favorite—disciplined, but with lots of spirit. Lacy Lu and Linney bonded instantaneously.

Cutter was riding a chestnut he called Sailor. It was apparent they were already fast friends by the way Sailor had perked up and trotted over to meet Cutter the second he came into view.

Linney followed Cutter's lead, trotting side by side for a while before letting the horses fly at full gallop. The speed was just the emotional release she needed, and the stress that had knotted her every muscle since Amy's death slowly fell away.

It was the first time Linney had been on a horse since she'd lived in Dobbin. In fact, the last time she'd ridden might have been here at the Double M the summer between her freshman and sophomore years at A&M.

Merlee had paid her to work as one of the counselors at a camp for underprivileged inner-city girls. It had been an eye-opening experience for Linney.

She'd been horrified at what some had told her about how they lived and shocked at their admitted sexual permissiveness while still in high school. Most of all, she'd been amazed at their resilience in the face of adversity. She'd laughed with many of them and cried with a few.

Linney had also spent an enormous amount of time hoping Cutter, who'd just graduated from UT and had taken a job in Austin would show up at the ranch for a visit. He hadn't.

Cutter slowed his horse as they reached the well-worn dirt path that led to a spring-fed stream on the northern edge of the Double M. She remembered the area well from her stint as a camp counselor. The girls had loved to go there and swim in the cool water on hot summer days.

When they reached the stream, Cutter let Sailor drink his fill, then dismounted and led the horse to the shade, tethering him to a low-hanging branch.

Linney followed suit, but the exhilarating freedom from stress she'd felt on the ride was slipping away fast. The tension building up inside her was different from before. This time it stemmed directly from Cutter. It zinged through her like electric current, leaving her tingling and on edge, as if something inside her might explode.

His hand brushed hers as he took Lacy Lu's reins

from her fingers, and she trembled at the sheer magnitude of the attraction. He hadn't done or said a thing to cause this crazy reaction in her at a time when she shouldn't be thinking of anything except getting justice for Amy.

It was just the effect of her thoughts and memories of their time together in California. A lot had happened since then. They weren't even the same people anymore. If they made love right here this minute, the passion would probably fall flat.

Cutter pulled an insulated pack and a small, rolled-up blanket from his saddlebags. "I brought cocktails," he said, "and some cheese and crackers. I thought we might as well have happy hour at the stream."

She swallowed hard. He was not making this easy.

He tossed her the blanket and she spread it on a carpet of pine straw near the water. She'd had lots of fantasies about Cutter over the years, starting when she was twelve and had her first serious crush on him. She remembered writing her name as Linney Gayle Martin on every spare scrap of paper in her school notebook.

Cutter set out the cheese and crackers and handed her a stapled set of papers. "You might want to take a look at this while we're out here," he said. "It's not exactly conducive to a relaxing happy hour, but I thought the content might go down for you more easily out here."

She glanced at page one and the heated, wanton memories fizzled and died.

Cutter poured a few fingers of amber liquid into a plastic cup and handed it to her.

She put it to her nose and sniffed. The sharp odor attacked her sinuses. "You know I hate whiskey."

She scanned the four pages of downloads, then wadded the papers into a tight ball and threw them as far as she could.

"I'm sorry, Linney, really sorry to have to show you that, but I thought you'd want to know the truth."

"Did you find out all of this just from the time you spent on the computer this afternoon?"

"Not all of it. Goose discovered the arrest records and the aliases. Given that information and the videos left at your house, the rest was easy to track down."

The facts were revolting, but they didn't change anything. So Amy wasn't the sweet, innocent victim she'd seemed. So she'd been arrested and jailed in Boston on charges of prostitution under the alias of Jo Jo Rottica. So she'd made a string of X-rated movies under various screen names that were still in circulation. So she'd been busted for possession of illegal narcotics on more than one occasion.

"That all happened when she was younger," Linney said, thinking aloud. "Amy had moved past that. She was a wonderful mother. And no matter what she'd done, she didn't deserve to be murdered."

"I couldn't agree more." Cutter slipped an arm around her shoulders.

She pulled away, downed the whiskey in one gulp and shoved the glass at him. "Hit me again."

He refilled the glass.

She sipped more slowly this time, relishing the burn as it slid down her throat and hit her rolling stomach. This was why Edna didn't want her daughter investigated. She knew this would come out. Dane must know all this as well. He'd had the same opportunities as Goose to check out Amy's background.

Still he'd married her, which didn't make a lot of sense, unless... "Dane.may have not have discovered the truth about Amy's past until after he married her and then took her past out on her with his fists."

"Or he may have discovered that Julie wasn't his child."

"Why would you say that? Do you know something I don't?" She exhaled sharply. "Of course you do. You're just a bundle of information today."

"I just have the date Amy and Dane were married. If the birthday party you went to for Julie was on or around her actual third birthday, then Amy was several months' pregnant when they got married."

"Oh, great. Poor Julie. She may not even have one living biological parent left. Actually that might be better than dealing with the fact that your father killed your mother."

"You keep forgetting innocent till proven guilty."

"Give it up, Cutter. Dane killed her and he tried to kill me, and the bastard is probably going to get away with all of it." The pent-up frustration and fury swelled until she felt as if her head were going to explode and go hurtling into space.

She needed an escape valve, some kind of emotional relief short of ripping out her own hair by the roots or beating her head against the ground. Only one came to mind.

Her fingers clutched the hem of her scoop-necked T-shirt and she yanked it over her head in one quick motion. Letting it fall to the ground, she kicked it out of the way along with her sandals.

Cutter was staring at her as if she'd lost her mind. Let him. She was past embarrassment and modesty. Slipping her fingers beneath her waistband, she unsnapped her denim shorts. They skimmed her legs and fell over her bare feet.

Then, without a backward glance, she marched to the edge of the water, wearing only her red lacy bra and matching thong panties. The mud curled around her toes and minnows played between her legs as she waded into the water and started to swim.

It was several minutes before her mind slowed and her agitation calmed enough for her to fully grasp that she'd just stripped in front of Cutter. He'd let her, just standing there without saying a word, not that he could have stopped her at that point.

But eventually, she'd have to get out of the stream in nothing more than a pair of see-through panties and a dripping-wet bra. Red, no less. Oh, well, he'd seen her in less.

She finally got up the nerve to stop swimming and let her feet touch bottom while she looked back at Cutter. He was still staring at her. Only now he was un-buttoning his shirt. He was coming in.

Her chest constricted as shudders of guilt shadowed the giddy anticipation that hit full force. She shouldn't feel this kind of thrill when Amy had been murdered only days before. But, right or wrong, she'd never needed a man more than she needed the gorgeous ex–Navy SEAL coming her way right now.

Chapter Nine

To his credit, Cutter was not so turned on that he didn't realize that going into the water with Linney would mean breaking all the rules he'd established for himself as far as she was concerned.

He knew that he'd eventually regret any kind of intimacy with her—even a kiss. She was just too damn hard to get over. He might be as tough and as disciplined as the SEAL program could make him, but he was still a man.

He stopped worrying with the buttons on his shirt and yanked it open, propelling the plastic disks in all directions. Then he made quick work of toeing out of his boots and wriggling out of his jeans and briefs.

The hesitancy was over. If he was going in, he was going in no holds barred.

His body was rock hard as he headed toward Linney. She had stopped swimming and was walking toward him, the water riding just below the soaked red bra that left nothing to the imagination. She was gorgeous. That was a given, but it didn't begin to explain why he'd never been able to shake her from his mind or dislodge her from his dreams.

He opened his arms as he neared her, and she hurled

herself into them. He slipped and they went under the water. When they surfaced, his mouth was on hers. Desire exploded inside him, and he claimed her lips, wanting all of her, one beautiful heart-stopping thrill at a time.

LINNEY'S BODY SEEMED LIGHTER than air and she felt as if she were floating somewhere a million miles from earth. The only thing that was real was Cutter. She clung to him, splaying the fingers of her left hand across his back while her right tangled in his hair.

Cutter's mouth and tongue ravaged hers and his need was exhilarating. She didn't want the kiss to end and she thrust against him until the need for air overpowered the passion.

She broke away only to have her senses skyrocket as he slipped his right hand between her thighs. His fingers rode up until they brushed her panties and the hard length of his erection nudged against her belly.

Her pulse pounded. The world stopped moving. It was only her and Cutter.

As his lips were searing a path down the column of her neck, tiny moans gurgled deep in her throat. She struggled to keep them silent. A word or even a sound might burst the magic and send her crashing back to the world of murder and heartbreak she'd just escaped.

He nudged his mouth beneath the silky border of her bra and found her right nipple with his lips. Pleasure swept through her, burning so deep inside her that trickles of hot, moist desire flowed from her core.

"Oh, Cutter. It's been so long."

"I never noticed."

He was a terrible liar.

He fit his hands inside her panties and pushed them over her hips. She helped him finish the job, releasing the delicate red puff of silk to float away in the blue water.

"Damn."

Cutter's guttural curse felt like a slap until... "Protection," she murmured, realizing why the urgency had cooled so quickly. "We don't have any."

"It's not that. It's Aurelio."

"What?"

"Shh. Listen."

She did and heard the clattering rumble of the pickup truck coming their way. She swallowed the howl of frustration that clogged her throat. They'd practically been caught in the act. The flames of passion cooled to the slow burn of mortification.

"How do you know it's Aurelio?"

"Training and instinct. I recognize the distinct sounds of the engine's clatter." Before he'd finished the sentence, the truck was in view.

Linney ducked so that just her neck and head were above the water. Cutter seemed unperturbed and as in control as ever. He was walking toward the bank and the water was already riding the tops of his hips.

"What's up?" he called, stopping his forward progress toward the bank within an inch of exposure.

"There are two men from the Green's Harbor Police Department here to see you. I thought you might want to talk to them, so I told them I'd try to find you. I can tell them I couldn't and try to get rid of them if you want."

"No." Linney answered for him. "It's important for me to talk to them. Make sure they don't leave before we get back."

"I don't think you've got a worry there. If they drove this far to see you, they're not going anywhere. Take all the time you need."

Meaning the obvious. Her cheeks burned.

"We'll be right there," Cutter said.

"I guess someone finally took the trouble to read my

complaint," Linney said as the foreman drove away. "Maybe now we'll get some action."

"I thought we had some pretty good action going on before Aurelio arrived."

Cutter strode away, leaving her the view of his masculine back side, all the way from his broad shoulders to his narrowing waist, right down to his hard buttocks and muscular thighs.

She'd deal with what had—or hadn't—happened between them later. Getting justice for Amy had to be her main focus now.

CUTTER STUDIED THE TWO OFFICERS sitting in the family room of the old ranch house. The youngest, Wesley Evans, looked to be in his late thirties and had identified himself as a homicide detective. Cutter suspected that his ties to Dane Colley were tight.

The second officer was Saul Prentiss, none other than the chief of police. Green's Harbor was a small town, but the man must have taken Linney's report seriously enough to drive all the way out to Dobbin himself. That or else he just didn't want to chance any bad publicity.

Cutter would guess the chief to be in his mid-forties, with a receding hairline and a slight paunch at the waist.

"How did you know where to find me?" Linney asked as she led the two men inside the house.

"We tried to reach you on your cell phone, and when we—"

"My cell phone never rang," Linney interrupted. She pulled it from the clip at her waist and flipped it open. "No network coverage," she admitted. She frowned. "So how did you find me?"

"We stopped by your house. Alfred Kingston was there and he said you'd left earlier with Cutter Martin."

"What was Al doing at my house?"

"Just sitting in your driveway when we arrived. He suggested we try to reach you at the Double M ranch in Dobbin. We drove out and a man working at the service station down the highway gave us directions to the ranch."

"And you drove all the way out here to follow up on Linney's complaints?" Cutter let his skepticism suffuse his tone. Unless police work had changed a hell of a lot while he'd been out of the country, the police would never be this diligent on a case they'd already closed.

"We can talk in here," he said, stopping in the large family room and motioning for them to take a seat.

The men took the sofa and immediately set the tenor of the meeting by sporting intimidating stares. Linney took an overstuffed armchair across from them, leaning back and crossing her long, shapely legs. Not intentionally seductive, but Cutter could tell that the move got the men's attention. Cutter propped himself up on the chair's arm.

"You wouldn't have had to track me down in Dobbin if you'd responded sooner to my concerns," Linney said, her tone every bit as daunting as their stares. "If that's an indication of how you run the rest of the department, then I can see why your investigation of the drowning was so shoddy."

Wesley sneered. "Our investigation was painstakingly meticulous and according to procedure."

And they were off.

Cutter geared up for the fireworks as he sized up the men and tried to figure out exactly why they'd suddenly decided to make the hour-plus drive to Dobbin after ignoring Linney's complaint for days.

"I read the report of your suspicions," the chief said, "but I'd like for you tell me in your own words exactly why you think Amy Colley was murdered and why her husband would commit such an act."

"Gladly. For starters, Dane Colley physically abused his wife. Amy had planned to leave him that very day."

Wesley seethed openly. "Dane? Physically abusive? That's a crock."

"She was bruised from where he'd punched her the day she drowned."

"She may have been bruised, but Dane didn't do it. And as for Amy threatening to leave him, she pulled that on him every time they had an argument. Dane knew she wouldn't follow through on it. They were both hot-tempered, but they loved each other."

"The way he'd love a punching bag." Linney's swinging foot went into high gear. "Dane killed Amy and you're covering up for him just because you're both cops."

Wesley's eyes narrowed. "Dane's a damn good cop, and your claims are preposterous."

Saul glared at Wesley as if he were ready to use a little physical force himself if Wesley didn't cool it. "Let's start over," Saul said, "and this time let's all try to stay calm. Mrs. Kingston, why don't you tell us when you last talked to Amy and how you got the idea that she planned to leave Dane?"

Mrs. Kingston. The name ground in Cutter's gut along with all the other irritants that were having a field day there.

"He not only killed Amy, he tried to kill me the other night."

"We had a call from a detective with the Houston Police Department concerning that," Saul said.

"And you damn sure can't connect that to Dane—if it even happened," Wesley said. "He was at a crime scene at the time and at least a dozen cops will swear to it."

He forced his focus back to Wesley while Linney gave the officers the details. The guy was nice-looking in a Bruce Willis, *Die Hard,* way. Not that Cutter was impressed, but he figured a lot of women would be.

The detective was all but spitting nails now, anger bunching his muscles and resentment firing from his dark eyes. Either he was the kind of cop who stood by a fellow officer no matter what or he was genuinely convinced of Dane's innocence.

Still, he'd reacted so quickly and so vehemently to the claims of abuse that Cutter had a feeling he knew they were true. On the other hand, Saul's face and eyes gave away little of what he was thinking.

The chief waited until Linney had finished talking before he spoke again. "I want you to know that we never take any citizen's concern lightly, Mrs. Kingston. I know that you were a close friend of Amy's and that's why I personally wanted to follow up on this."

"I'm glad someone finally followed up on it," Linney said, cutting him no slack.

Saul rubbed his chin. "I talked to the officer who responded to Dane's call when he found his wife floating in the pool. He claims his report is accurate and that there were absolutely no traces of evidence suggesting her death was the result of foul play."

"And Dane has an alibi," Wesley said. "Ironclad, easily verified by a half-dozen new recruits to the department and any number of police officers and clerical staff who were in the building where he was teaching classes that morning."

"*Ironclad* is a pretty strong term," Cutter said, breaking in for the first time.

Wesley crossed his arms in front of him and jutted his craggy jaw. "Detective Colley was accounted for every second."

Cutter stood and moved behind Linney's chair. "I understand the classes were conducted in an annex less than five minutes from Dane's home. That means he could have made a trip there and back in the time it would take to…say, take a bathroom break."

"A good point," Saul agreed, "but surveillance cameras in the parking lot prove that Dane's car never left the lot."

"Dane might have borrowed someone else's car," Cutter said, "maybe one not parked in the lot."

The chief nodded. "That's possible. Not likely."

"Because you say so?"

"No, because Dane's one of our best officers. I've never had a reason to doubt anything he's said before, and there was no evidence of a crime."

"But the autopsy report did show a trauma to the head and several bruises on the body in various stages of fading," Cutter said, "many in areas that wouldn't be seen if she were wearing normal street clothes."

"Do you have a point to make?" Wesley asked.

"I just made it," Cutter said. "That pattern of repeated bruising is considered an indicator of possible physical abuse."

Saul scratched his chin. "I see you've done your homework, Mr. Martin, though I'm not sure how you gained access to the autopsy report."

The chief's response told him that Linney had most likely called the abuse factor right.

"People who have seizures show the same patterns of bruising," Wesley said. "And the blow to the head was consistent with Amy's having tripped on the overturned lounge before falling into the water."

"Amy didn't fall," Linney said, her temper pushing her voice an octave higher than usual. "She was hit or pushed. And Amy didn't have seizures."

"Call it whatever you want to," Wesley said. "I was at their house one night when her eyes turned glassy and she started shaking. A few seconds later she went limp and if Dane hadn't caught her, she'd have fallen and likely hit her head on the concrete patio."

"Wesley and Dane are partners," Saul explained, "two of the department's most experienced homicide detectives."

"Then I guess you'd better start looking for a new ace detective to partner with," Linney said, "because before this is over, Dane Colley is going to prison, hopefully for life."

"If he's guilty, then I hope you're right," Saul said, "but to be honest with you, I'm ninety-nine percent positive you're imagining guilt where none exists. Amy's drowning was unfortunate, but all the evidence we have, including lack of motive and opportunity on Dane's part, indicates that her death was an accident."

"You have motive," Linney said. "Amy was going to leave Dane."

"We only have your word for that."

"Why would I lie?"

"I don't know, but there were no packed bags at her house or in her car. And no booked flights except the one to Las Vegas where she and Dane were going in two weeks to celebrate their anniversary," Chief Prentiss said.

"Then she agreed to that trip before she decided to leave him."

"The reservations were made the Thursday night before she drowned."

"She was afraid of Dane. If she agreed to the trip, it was to keep him from going ape on her and punching her again."

But Cutter could tell that the chief's last statement had stolen a lot of Linney's thunder. Which was no doubt exactly what they'd intended when they'd driven all the way out here.

Even the mix of personalities had likely been orchestrated. Good police chief and angry partner of the cop Linney was accusing of murder. Together they would sell her the total innocence package.

Maybe Amy's drowning *was* an accident, though Cutter doubted it. But if it was, then who had come gunning for Linney and why? Those were the questions Cutter couldn't let go of, nor was he ready to write Al Kingston out of the equation.

At this point the pieces of the puzzle were all twisted, with jagged edges that defied a solution. His leg started to throb as the tension took hold.

Gather all the facts. That was a major rule of readying for a new operation, and he obviously didn't have the full picture yet. But as he escorted the police chief and the resentful detective to the door, an idea for how to proceed started kicking around in his mind.

"YOU CANNOT BREAK INTO a cop's house."

"I'm pretty sure I can, Linney. I've crossed enemy lines on land, parachuted into Taliban strongholds and maneuvered underwater assault craft beneath the cover of ocean currents. I don't think getting past a locked door will be much of a challenge."

Linney stared at Cutter, irritated that he was even considering this kind of crazy move. "If Dane finds you in his house, he won't think twice before shooting you."

"He won't find me."

"You can't be sure of that. Evidently, he pops into the house whenever he chooses. To kill his wife. To shoot intruders. Anyway, I don't know what you think you'd find inside the house that would help."

"Missing pieces to the puzzle."

"Like what? Amy died outside, in the pool, just as

Dane planned. There won't even be spots of blood on the carpet or splattered across the walls."

"There might be other evidence, such as messages left on the answering machine, a call log, Amy's laptop."

"If there was anything incriminating left inside the house, Dane's had plenty of time to get rid of it."

"The death was ruled an accident. There was no need for him to give evidence a second thought."

Linney nodded and took a deep breath as she realized that Cutter was making sense. They needed something specific to tie Dane to the murder. Otherwise, it was just her word against his and his alibi.

"Amy's laptop could help," she admitted. "I know she kept an online calendar for all her appointments. She may have made reservations at a hotel for Friday night or even corresponded with someone about a job in a different area."

"I'd also like to know why your ex-husband was back at your house," Cutter said. "And how he knows about the Double M."

"Forget Al. He probably just figured he'd have a better chance of playing on my sympathies if he caught me home alone. And I pointed out the Double M to him last year when we went to Dobbin for a friend's wedding. I told him you were our famous Navy SEAL neighbor."

Al was the least of her worries now. "So when do we go snooping?" she asked.

"*I* go snooping tomorrow."

"You don't seriously think I'm staying here while you do my dirty work for me."

"No. You'll stay with Goose."

"I don't need a babysitter, Cutter."

"Right. You need a bodyguard, and Goose is probably the most capable person for that in the Houston area—next to me, of course."

So he had this all worked out in his mind before he'd even mentioned it to her. Like she was some irresponsible bimbo who'd been thrust upon him. Yet he hadn't kissed her like she was a bimbo back at the swimming hole.

Heat flooded her body as the memories of their brief encounter took hold. She was falling for Cutter all over again, if she'd ever really gotten over him. She wanted to make love to him, wanted to feel his arms around her, wanted to let the passion have full sway.

But not if this was just part of his readjustment process before he moved on with his life. She'd been on that route and she wasn't going there again.

"Why are you doing this, Cutter?"

"I told you. We need answers. This is a sensible next move."

"No, I mean why are you putting your life and future on the line for a situation I just threw in your lap? Is this about me or Amy or about you needing to be a hero? Forgive me if I sound ungrateful. I'm just trying to get some perspective here."

He shoved his hands into the front pockets of his jeans and exhaled slowly. "I don't really know how to answer that. A little of all of the above, I guess."

"That's not good enough."

"Then try this. I didn't ask to get involved in this, but now that I'm in it, I'm going to finish what I started and that includes keeping you safe."

She could live with that for now. "I'm going with you, Cutter, but we won't have to resort to breaking and entering. I still have the key Amy gave me a few weeks back when I picked up Julie from day care while she was having some dental work done. If Dane comes by, I can say I stopped in to pick up some things for Julie."

Cutter shrugged. "We'll talk about it tomorrow."

The answer was more a dismissal than an agreement.

An hour ago, she'd been in his arms, hungry for his kisses, aching for fulfillment. He'd seemed every bit as hot for her as she was for him. Now even being in the same room seemed awkward. And still…

"I'll be in my room if you need me," she said.

She had little hope that he would.

IT WAS JUST AFTER eleven p.m. when Dane picked up the black plastic bag. The trash was only shreds of Amy's betrayal, yet it felt like bones he was tossing into the backseat of his car.

He'd made lots of mistakes in his life. Amy had been the biggest. He'd known she'd be trouble the night he met her, knew he should have screwed her brains out and walked away.

But she had that way about her, a devastating blend of seductiveness and vulnerability that had sucked him in like a killer twister. He'd loved her. But he had never been the one she wanted. Second best took its toll on a man.

Cruel. Abusive. Threatening. Easy terms for a woman like Linney Kingston to throw around. But what did she know about the way a woman like Amy could drive a man crazy? It wasn't that he'd enjoyed hitting her. She'd driven him to it.

It was finally over now.

He went back into the house to get the keys to his car. He could use his own trash can, but just to be on the safe side, he'd drive to the dumpster behind the strip mall on Harbor Drive. He'd make no mistakes, leave nothing to chance.

His chest constricted as he neared the door to the master bedroom. He tried to keep walking, but his legs ground to a halt and he was left to peer at the bed he'd never share with Amy again.

His mind played cruel tricks on him, replaying

images that were so potent he could smell Amy's perfume and hear her voice. A sharp pain stabbed him in the chest. He fell against the doorframe, afraid he was having a heart attack. Before he could react to the emergency, Amy's image faded and the throbbing subsided.

What's done was done. Only the strong survive. Dane was made of granite. Amy had said so herself.

THE GRANDFATHER CLOCK in the hallway finished its twelfth bong as Cutter walked past the master suite. There was no line of light shining beneath the door and no sounds coming from the room. Apparently, Linney was sleeping.

He should be doing the same, but sleep never came easily when his mind was running full throttle, the way it was now. He understood Linney's dedication to getting justice for her friend and her concern that Julie's custody would be in the hands of the man who'd killed her mother. He'd do his best to get to the bottom of it.

More pressing at the moment was that someone wanted Linney dead. The attempt on her life had not been a random act. He had to identify the culprit, but there were too damn many questions without answers.

And far too many emotions without an outlet.

Neither his mind nor his body had recovered from this afternoon's encounter. He couldn't look at Linney without tasting her lips and feeling the press of her body against his. He couldn't think of her without his emotions taking off in wanton tangents and the ache inside him swelling to the point that it was all he could do not to just throw her onto the nearest surface and take her like some savage barbarian.

The six years he'd spent telling himself that what he'd felt in San Diego had been no more than release from his exhaustive weeks of BUD/S had dissolved the second she started shedding her clothes. Wanting her was all wrong. She was too damn hard to get over when she finished with him.

But he wanted her so desperately that just thinking about her was making him rock hard and steaming up his mind. He hurried the last few steps, kicking out of his shoes and unbuttoning his shirt the second he stepped into his room. He needed a cold shower in the worst way.

He stood beneath the spray for several minutes after the soapy film from a rough scrubbing was long gone down the drain. He'd just stepped onto the fluffy mat when he heard the tentative knock on the bedroom door. He'd intentionally left it ajar so that he could hear any sounds inside the house.

Grabbing the generously sized green towel, he pulled it about him. Still dripping, he stuck his head around the bathroom door.

"Cutter, I just thought of—"

Linney was standing inside his bedroom in a pair of black silk pajamas. He stared, totally bewitched and unaware that she'd stopped talking. Finally, he managed to come to his senses enough to realize that she was staring at the erection that stretched the towel into a new shape.

"What did you want to tell me?"

"I don't remember." Her voice had a breathless quality that sent him into orbit. He let go of the towel and let it fall. He'd pay the devil later. Tonight he was heaven-bound.

Chapter Ten

Linney stood motionless, anticipation running hot inside her. Cutter Martin was standing in front of her, naked, magnificent as a virile god who'd been sent here to pleasure all her senses.

He crossed the room in a heartbeat and took her in his arms. His lips came down on hers, brutal, ravaging, thrilling. Passion exploded inside her and she kissed him back just as hungrily. Their tongues collided and tangled and their bodies pressed against each other, soft against hard, hollows against swells. Heat against heat.

The kiss grew deeper still as his hand slid between her legs. Sensations vibrated inside her. She loved his touch even through the silky pajamas, but she wished she were naked, too. She ached to feel his flesh against hers.

His mouth pushed against the fabric, moving it back from her cleavage until his lips skimmed her right breast. Her nipples came to life, suddenly bursting with feeling and straining for release.

"Undress me," she whispered.

A rasping cry was all he managed in answer as he slipped his rough hands beneath her pajama top and pulled it over her head. She tugged at the waistband of the pants, ready to finish stripping herself.

He took her hands in his. "Let me," he said. Only he didn't. Instead he cupped her breasts and let his thumbs massage the nipples until they were ripe and pebbled and aching to be kissed. He obliged, sucking one breast, exploring the other and then reversing the action as if each nipple required ample attention.

Desire rocked her body from the inside out. She'd thought she remembered everything about making love to Cutter, but she'd forgotten how intoxicating his touch was, forgotten how he made every inch of her body an erogenous playground.

He kissed her nipples, her stomach, her navel, and the soft flesh inside the curves of her arms. Finally, he picked her up and carried her to his bed. With one swift move, he threw back the quilt and laid her on top of the crisp white sheets.

She stretched out and he straddled her, his fingers finally slipping below the waistband of her pajama bottoms. She fought the urge to wriggle out of them quickly and let the slow burn consume her as he inched them down slowly. His lips found her navel and then trailed lower as he fit his knee between her thighs and opened her for his touch.

By the time the pajamas had cleared her feet and he'd thrown them to the floor, she was miles beyond needing him. She took his erection in her hand and stroked, growing hotter still as he moaned in pleasure.

She thrust toward him as she guided his hard length to her. "I want you inside me, Cutter. All of you."

"Oh, Linney, how do you do this to me?"

"Do what?"

"Make me crazy with wanting you."

"I like you crazy, Cutter. Crazy for me."

He reached to the nightstand and fumbled for the condom he'd optimistically left there earlier that day. In seconds, he'd stretched it over his erection. He pushed inside her and the last remnants of control vanished. She thrust with him, biting her lip to keep from screaming as the rush of molten fire surged through her. The thrill was so intense it hurt.

And then she felt his body tremble and she pushed hard, going over the top with him, every cell in her body igniting in that one second of complete and wanton passion.

Cutter lowered his head and let himself back down on her gently, his breath so ragged it seemed to be tearing from his lungs. The words *I love you* were flying around in her heart, but when she tried to say them, they became trapped on her tongue.

She'd said *"I love you"* six years ago. She'd meant the words with all her heart when she'd said them. But they'd hung in the air like an air kiss, empty if no one said them back. Cutter hadn't said them then and she was almost sure he wouldn't say them now. He loved making love to her. She loved *him*.

She'd tried for six years to convince herself that the California rendezvous had been about lust and need, an extension of the crush she'd had on the most gorgeous and exciting boy in Dobbin, maybe in all of Texas.

But she'd never felt this way with anyone but Cutter. He made the magic. That's why the memories never dimmed and the desire never faded. But she couldn't bring herself to say "I love you" tonight.

They didn't talk at all, but she cuddled in Cutter's arms until his even breathing told her he'd fallen asleep. Then she closed her eyes and drifted into the first sound sleep she'd had since Amy's death.

LINNEY STRETCHED and opened her eyes to a sweet ache between her thighs and that drugged numbness that comes from hours of sound, restful sleep. She squirmed between the sheets as the full memory of last night's lovemaking settled into her bones.

Turning, she reached for Cutter. The spot where he'd slept was still warm, but vacant. Disappointment crawled inside her and she kicked free of the covers and slid her feet to the floor. The clock by the bed said 8:00 a.m., the latest she'd slept in days. No wonder Cutter had left her alone.

Still, waking up without him after the skyrockets and glorious fulfillment of last night left her with an incredible sense of emptiness. It was almost as if part of her were missing. Was it possible Cutter had felt that same way when she'd sneaked out of the motel room before he woke on their last morning in San Diego?

No way. They'd been dynamite together, the way they'd been last night. But no matter how deliciously thrilling their time together had been, it had been merely a jumping-off place for Cutter. He was on his way to becoming a SEAL. She was a diversion, a release from the ardors of training. The military was his life.

The rules had been clear then. Five days and he had to leave for the next part of his training. But the rules of engagement were muddled now, at least for her. There was no clear-cut road map for how this was supposed to continue—or to end.

She padded to the door, picking up her pajamas as she went. Her top had been on the floor last night. She vaguely remembered seeing the bottoms tangled in a bouquet of silk flowers on the table near the window. They were both neatly folded now and waiting on top of the Queen Anne dressing table.

Not bothering to put them on, she held them in front of her like a shield as she opened the door. The odor of fresh-brewed coffee and sizzling bacon enticed her to move quickly as she went to her own room to slip into something less revealing and more functional for a ranch breakfast.

Five minutes later, she joined Cutter in the kitchen. Her heart skipped a couple of beats at the sight of him. He had on a pair of faded jeans. That was it. No shirt. No shoes.

"Hope you're hungry," Cutter said, without turning around.

"Famished." She swallowed hard and her heart found its way back to a steady beat as an awkwardness took hold. Did she walk over and kiss him good-morning or play it like he hadn't shaken her world last night? She was saved from deciding by the scene that popped onto the screen of the under-the-counter TV.

Her ex-husband was smiling into the camera and speaking into a microphone that had been shoved into his face. Cutter noticed him as well and upped the volume.

"It's all a misunderstanding and I expect it to be cleared up as soon as the Treasury Department has all the facts. That's all I have to say at this time, but my attorney will answer any other questions you have."

The attorney took the next few questions, yelling foul on the part of the IRS and emphasizing his client's total innocence. Linney recognized the sharp-dressed, middle-aged attorney, but knew he was not part of Al's regular on-retainer legal team.

"My ex must be worried," she said as she poured herself a mug of strong, black coffee. "That was Marvin Valentine. He's one of the top defense attorneys in the state."

"The name sounds familiar."

"He's the one who got Reverend Pike's wife off after she admitted stabbing her two-timing evangelist husband six times while he was asleep."

"No wonder his name sounds familiar. Merlee kept me updated on all the details of that trial. She thought the good reverend deserved what he got."

"A lot of women did. Seems there's a limit to how many beautiful women you can 'counsel' before the wife is entitled to a temporary mental snap."

"Poor preacher," Cutter teased. "He was just trying to help the lonely widows."

"Yeah, right."

"Interesting, though, that Big Al feels he needs the state's most expensive lawyer to beat the case the Feds have against him," Cutter said. "He's either guilty or running scared."

"Doing time would kill him," she said. "No one to butter his bread or shine his eight hundred dollar Italian wingtips."

"Hate those dirty wingtips. How do you like your eggs?"

"Lightly scrambled. Why don't you let me do it?"

"I've got it under control, but you can get out the hot sauce. It's a staple after eating military food for so many years. And there's a collection of homemade jams in the fridge. Help yourself." He broke four eggs into a glass bowl. "Tell me more about Al."

Not her favorite breakfast topic. "Like what?"

"Does he have a temper?"

Back to that. "Probably no more than most men with his kind of money and clout. He expects to get his way and heads roll when he doesn't. But, as I've said, he wouldn't come after me with guns blazing the way that guy did the other night."

She was convinced that it would take a psychopath like Dane Colley to do that. She got the hot sauce and a jar of fig preserves and finished setting the table with paper napkins and Merlee's mismatched utensils.

"You said he was controlling," Cutter said, unwilling to drop the subject. "In what way?"

"Actually, I wouldn't have described him that way when we were first married, at least not as far as his relationship with me. By the end of the marriage he expected me to follow his dictates about everything from what I wore to the endless social events he insisted I attend. Even to the length of my hair."

"And if you didn't follow his dictates?"

"Then he stormed out and didn't speak to me, sometimes for days. Frankly, that was a blessing at times. I didn't have to listen to his endless complaints over his foreign business dealings. He was always certain he was being taken advantage of, though the money kept rolling in."

Cutter carried the plates of egg, bacon and buttered biscuits to the table. "But he was never violent?"

She hesitated, hating to lie, yet knowing Cutter would read the wrong thing into the truth. "He could be a tad violent if he was pushed too far."

Cutter dropped the second plate to the table with a bang. One of his biscuits fell from the plate. "He hit you, didn't he?"

"Only once."

Cutter's hands fisted and the muscles in his arms flexed as if preparing for a fight. "Tell me what happened."

"It's over and done with. There's no point in dealing with this now."

"Why did he hit you?" Cutter insisted.

"Someone was throwing a birthday party in his honor. It was a big deal. Everyone who's anyone, as he liked to say, was invited. The marriage was basically over, and I refused to go with him. I couldn't stand to continue the farce. He turned red in the face and punched me in the jaw. That's all there was to it."

"That two-bit son of a bitch. I hope you called the cops."

"I didn't."

"So you just let him get away with it?"

"No, I filed for legal separation the next day."

"Any man who hits a woman deserves to…" His words dissolved into muttered curses. "Didn't you see any of that when you couldn't wait to marry him?"

When she couldn't wait to marry him? The sarcasm was almost buried beneath Cutter's fury, but it was still there. He meant when she'd married Al only months after making love to Cutter. Right now Cutter was the one with an excess of gall.

"No, I didn't see the negative qualities in Al before I married him. Now can we please just drop this?"

Cutter let the subject die, but by then she'd lost her appetite. Not only that, but the heated glow from last night's lovemaking had cooled to a dull film covering her heart.

If she'd had some kind of half-baked notion that they could pick up where they'd left off and make it work this time, she was way off base.

She picked at her food, finally forcing down a few bites. Cutter on the other hand cleaned his plate. He seemed more preoccupied than irritated once the initial anger passed. Her mind went back to the problems at hand as well. Dane was still a free man and the concern she'd gone to Cutter's room to talk about last night continued to plague her mind.

"I'd like to stop by and see Amy's mother on the way into town this morning," she said.

Cutter went back for more coffee and refilled her cup as well. "We can do that, but I doubt she's going to tell you more than you already know about Amy."

"I know, but I keep thinking about what Julie said

about Dane hitting the bad man. I think it's relevant to her mother's death. Why else would it be the only thing she's said when she's so traumatized by Amy's drowning?" Despite her numerous attempts, Linney hadn't gotten anything more out of the child.

"I think it may take Julie's saying something to incriminate Dane before Edna would believe he may have killed her."

"I agree, though I don't understand why, unless Amy kept the abuse from her."

"That's very possible," Dane agreed. "You saw the bruises because she had to go to work. She could have easily made excuses not to see her mother when they were at their worst."

Linney carried the dishes to the sink. "While we're there, I'll offer to pick up whatever else she might need for Julie. Surely she's thought of something Dane forgot by now. That way we have a legitimate excuse for being inside the house if we're discovered."

"You don't listen very well, do you?"

Cutter was speaking in that authoritarian, rankling, military tone again. She wasn't under his command. "I listen just fine." She started to march away.

Cutter grabbed both her arms and tugged her around to face him. "You're a kindergarten teacher. You know kids far better than I do. Secret surveillance and invasion without detection are my areas of expertise. I'm not risking either one of us getting arrested or shot because you are too stubborn to listen to reason."

"So it's your way or not at all?"

"In this case."

He wasn't going to budge. His attitude was arrogant, determined, dogged. And unequivocally protective. She wanted to lash out at him but the truth was she'd never felt more safe and cared for in her life.

TO LINNEY'S SURPRISE, Edna seemed almost relieved to see them at her door. Her eyes were red and puffy, but she ushered them inside quickly. Insisting they join her for a glass of iced tea, she only told them there had been some new developments.

Linney's hope went shooting upward. It was past time they got a break.

Edna didn't supply any new information until she'd poured their tea and they were all sitting around a small round table in a windowed breakfast nook that overlooked a garden lush with summer blossoms.

Edna clasped her hands on the table. "I had a visit from two police officers last night."

"Saul Prentiss and Wesley Evans?" Cutter asked.

"Yes. How did you know?"

"They visited us as well," Linney said. "What did you tell them?"

Edna nervously worried a small silver bracelet on her left wrist. Linney knew the jewelry was a gift from Amy, a thank-you for her having kept Julie while they'd gone to a three-day teachers' convention in Dallas.

"I told them that I was satisfied that Amy's death was accidental, that I didn't suspect foul play."

No surprise, considering Edna's insistence yesterday that Linney not cause a stir. But if that's all that was said, Edna's comment about new developments made no sense.

"Wesley was ready to leave as soon as I said that," Edna explained. "Saul Prentiss had lots more questions, mostly about whether or not Dane had ever physically hurt Amy and if she'd mentioned the possibility of leaving Dane."

Good for the police chief. He was probably just looking for an excuse to drop Linney's complaint into file thirteen, but at least he was following up.

"I'm certain Dane hit Amy," Linney repeated for what seemed like the zillionth time.

"I guess I just wanted so badly to believe that Amy's marriage was working that I ignored any sign that it wasn't. But I would have been there for her if she'd told me. I always wanted to be there for her." Edna's voice broke and Linney knew she was fighting back tears.

She slid her hands across the table and wrapped them around Edna's. "I know all about Amy's past, Mrs. Sears. But that's just what it was—the past. She'd turned her life around. She didn't deserve to be abused and she definitely didn't deserve to be murdered."

"I guess it's just so hard for me to think Dane could kill her. He was jealous and possessive. I saw that in him, but I thought he loved her. And he's always been good to Julie."

"Maybe none of us knows the real Dane," Cutter suggested. "Maybe Amy didn't even know the full extent of what he was capable of."

"No. She knew."

Cutter pushed his glass away. "What brought you to that conclusion?"

"I was at my computer a few minutes ago, the first time since Amy's death. No, the first time since last Wednesday. I was checking my e-mail when Amy brought Julie out for a visit. She used the computer for a few minutes while she was here, but I never went back to it."

"Did you get an e-mail about Amy?" Linney asked, wondering where this was going.

"The e-mail wasn't to me. I was just staring at the new mail when I realized it wasn't mine, but Amy's. I guess she must have forgotten to log off when she was here last week so when I checked the mail, it was hers that came up."

Cutter propped his elbows on the table and leaned in close. "Are you saying you have access to Amy's e-mail?"

"Well, to one account anyway. It's not the account that I use when writing her."

Linney's pulse pounded. A secret e-mail account. This could be exactly what they needed. "Did you read her mail?"

"A few of the entries. I felt guilty spying on her that way, but I don't see how it can hurt now. And one of the e-mails that I read changes everything."

"How's that?" Cutter asked.

"She told someone with the screen name of Drbil that she was afraid Dane was planning to kill her."

"We need to see that e-mail," Linney said.

"I was planning to call Chief Prentiss."

"Better to let us take a look at it first," Cutter said. "The chief will likely confiscate the computer as evidence and then the police will be the only ones with access to the messages."

"Chief Prentiss assured me that he'd conduct a full investigation if it was warranted."

"The sad truth is that the police have been known to cover up for one of their own," Cutter said.

The understatement of the year, especially if Wesley Evans or Dane Colley got their hands on the incriminating evidence.

"I suppose you could be right," Edna conceded. "I know that Wesley Evans and Dane are very close. The few times I've been to Amy's for dinner, Wesley has been there, too, either for the meal or just to drop by. Amy liked him, too. She always seemed to laugh more when he was around."

"Where's the computer?" Linney asked, eager to read the incriminating e-mails.

"In the spare bedroom." Edna stood just as the doorbell rang. "It's probably a delivery. I have a weakness for the shopping channel," she said, smiling surreptitiously.

The woman most definitely had an overactive guilt complex—and an incredibly naive concept of cops. "Lucky we stopped by when we did," Linney whispered to Cutter as Edna hurried to the front door. "If Wesley Evans had gotten his hands on this information, I doubt it would have ever surfaced again."

Loud voices came from the doorway. Linney rushed into the hallway for a better look. Her optimism plunged. It wasn't a deliveryman at the door. It was the infamous cop duo of Dane Colley and Wesley Evans. And judging from the sound of his voice, Dane was furious.

Chapter Eleven

"Don't lie to me, Edna. I know that's Cutter Martin's truck parked out front."

"It's my house, Dane. I can have anyone I want here."

Cutter stepped between Edna and Dane. "And if you have a problem with that, Detective, take it up with me."

Dane stuck out his jaw and doubled both hands into fists. "I'll be glad to."

Linney tugged Edna away so that she wouldn't be in harm's way if punches started to fly. Dane looked as if he was about to explode, and she had no doubt that Cutter would stand up to him if things came to blows.

"I know all about you, Cutter. Big SEAL hero. Well, that's not worth two cents around here. Stay out of my life or I'll give you so much trouble you'll wish you were in a war zone."

"Are you afraid of what I'll find, Detective? Because you sure act like a man with something to hide."

"Go to hell! And as for you, Linney, Amy would be mortified at your behavior. She thought you were her friend."

"I was."

"Is that why you're so hell-bent on making a circus of her death?"

"I want justice."

"Bull!"

"That's enough," Cutter said. "You got a problem with me, that's fine, but leave Linney out of this."

"Then keep her out of my life. Amy's dead and I'm not going to have her name dragged through the mud just because your girlfriend has some crazy idea that I killed my wife."

"Doesn't seem so crazy to me," Cutter said, "seeing as how you're so adamantly opposed to any kind of investigation."

Wesley raked his unruly coal-black hair from his brow and turned toward Edna. "Don't tell me you're buying in to their bizarre accusations, Mrs. Sears. You know how much Dane loved Amy. You know how hard this has been on him."

Edna's hand slid down the door and she dropped her arm to her side, almost as if the fight had been sucked from her. "I don't know anything anymore. All I know is that Amy's gone forever." Her eyes moistened.

"You know what will happen if the news media gets hold of this case and starts digging into Amy's background," Dane said. "Is that what you want? Is that the kind of memories you want Julie to carry of her mother?"

What gall. But this was taking things too far. Linney pushed in front of Cutter. "Is that the threat you used to keep Amy from leaving you when you punched her? That you'd tell Julie her mother was an ex–porn star?"

"You bitch."

"Let's take this outside," Cutter said, his tone making it clear that he'd had enough.

Edna started to shake. She took a step forward and shook her fist in Dane's face. "Get out, Dane. Get out of my house."

Dane drew back a fist but moved toward Cutter.

Wesley grabbed his arm and held him back. "Settle down, buddy. He's not worth bruising your hand over."

"You're right." Dane broke away from Wesley's grasp and turned his burning glare toward Edna. "I'm not going anywhere until I see my daughter."

"My neighbor took Julie to the park with her two children. She needed some fresh air and to be around other kids."

Dane shoved his hands into his pockets. "Fine, but get rid of Linney and Cutter. If I find out they've been here again, I'll take Julie home with me and it's the last you'll see of your granddaughter."

The guy was full of threats, all of which made him look even guiltier. Hopefully, Edna saw that, too. At least she hadn't caved and told Dane and Wesley about the e-mails.

Cutter stepped outside as they left, standing on the small portico as the two men returned to a black unmarked sedan.

"Poor Julie," Edna said. "My poor, sweet Julie."

Linney put her arm around Edna's stooped shoulders. It had been hard enough on her when she thought her daughter's death had been an accident. Now she had to face the possibility that her son-in-law was a murderer and all the added complications that would heap on her granddaughter.

"I'm glad you were here when they came by," Edna said, when the sedan had sped away and Cutter rejoined them. "Seeing all that fury in Dane makes the e-mail a lot more credible. You'll see what I mean when you read it." She started back down the hallway with them a step behind.

JULIE RETURNED FROM THE PARK just as Edna pulled up the e-mail that she'd found so disturbing—the only one in the inbox from Drbil. Edna left to tend her young charge, leaving Linney and Cutter on their own.

Linney read the note out loud. "'So why are you still with that bastard? Get out of that house! I'm worried sick about you. If you want me to come for you, just say the word. I can be there within hours.'"

But it was the note that Drbil had responded to that made Linney's blood run cold. It was included in the e-mail along with the date it had been sent. Late Wednesday afternoon, less than forty-eight hours before Amy's death.

I don't know how he found out, but I think Dane knows that I'm planning to leave him. He didn't speak to me at all this morning and when I asked him if he'd be home for dinner, he just stared back at me with a threatening look. It sent chills through me. For the first time, I really think he may be planning to kill me.

Linney shivered as she reread the message. "No wonder Amy seemed so nervous that last day at the café. I should have said more. I should have insisted that she come home with me. If I had, she'd still be alive."

"You had no way of knowing, but even if you had, I doubt you could have changed anything. She feared that he might kill her and yet she spent the night in that house. And we still don't have proof that she was actually murdered."

"Maybe not enough proof for a jury," Linney said, "but this e-mail is more than enough for me."

"Do you think Drbil is man or woman?"

"A man, definitely a man."

"Why? There's nothing to indicate that."

"He wants to come to her rescue. That sounds manly."

"You're berating yourself for not coming to her rescue," Cutter said. "I'm sure her mother is, too. Drbil may just be a good female friend she felt she could confide in."

"Good point. Keep looking for messages. Try the sent and deleted files."

"No obvious tracks," Cutter said, as he scanned all possible file folders. "Amy was careful to destroy all correspondence from Drbil, at least on this computer."

"Isn't there some way you can recover that information from the hard drive?"

"Sometimes. I have a friend in Dallas who's a specialist in forensic computer analysis. I'll get him to take a look at it, unless Goose knows someone here in Houston. But then we may not need the information if we locate Amy's computer and we get enough evidence from it."

"We should take it with us," Linney said. "I'm sure Edna will agree to that."

"Good idea."

"I'm thinking Amy may not have written to Drbil on her computer at all for fear that Dane would find out. That's why she used her mother's computer to send this message to him."

Cutter went back to the message and hit the Reply button. "You do the honors," he said, vacating the chair in front of the keyboard. "Say you were Amy's friend and that you urgently need to talk to him or her."

Linney composed as she typed, explaining how Edna had located this e-mail and that she needed to speak with him as soon as possible regarding Amy. Then she added her cell phone number.

She took a deep breath and hit Send just as Edna appeared in the doorway.

"I'm sure you can see why I was so disturbed by the e-mail."

"Most definitely," Linney said. "I replied to the sender

and gave him my phone number and e-mail address. Hopefully, we'll hear back."

"Whoever it was, Amy apparently trusted him more than she trusted me," Edna said. "We were connecting again, but for years we didn't speak. It was hard for us to get past all that."

"I'm sure she knew you loved her," Linney said. "Sometimes it's just easier to confide in an old friend than in family."

"I guess. I'm going to the kitchen to fix Julie a peanut-butter-and-jelly sandwich. She always has lunch at eleven and I don't like to toy with her schedule, especially now. Can I get you something?"

"Nothing for me," Cutter said.

Linney turned down the offer as well. Reading the e-mail had left her queasy.

Edna started to leave, then hesitated. "You're lucky to have Cutter, Linney. Hold on to him. Men like that are hard to find."

And even harder to hold on to. Memories of last night came crashing down on Linney without warning and she stared at the computer for fear that the emotional roller-coaster ride she was on would show on her face.

She had no idea where she stood with Cutter. When he'd made love to her, it was as if she were the only woman on earth, as if he couldn't get enough of her. Now it was as if they were merely partners investigating a crime.

Not even equal partners at that. He called the shots when it suited him to do so. He'd break in to Amy and Dane's house. She'd be left with a sitter.

But he was here, giving up his days and nights because she'd asked him to. And because he thought she needed protection, so much so that he wouldn't even let her stay alone while he searched the Colley house for evidence.

Her hero. And the one man who could break her heart all over again.

Cutter's cell phone rang. "It's Goose," he said as he checked the caller ID. "I need to take it."

She nodded and let her gaze return to the unnerving e-mail as he stepped from the room. She wondered what he had to say to Goose that he couldn't say in front of her.

She made six copies of the e-mail—insurance in case the original disappeared into cyberspace. Once they were folded and tucked neatly into the back pocket of her capris, she went upstairs to find Julie and say hello.

She heard her before she saw her.

"No. No. No. Don't hurt him. Please don't hurt him."

The voice was haunting, like a tiny version of Amy's. Linney hurried to the only door in the hall that stood ajar. Before she entered, she spied Julie's reflection in the mirror over the dresser.

The child was sitting on the floor acting out the scene with her dolls and stuffed animals. The bear was pounding the smaller lion cub with his whole body. The doll was in her left hand standing over the other two.

"Stop it, Dane. Stop it! Let him go." Julie started to whimper as if the doll were crying. Then Julie threw and kicked both stuffed animals, sending them skidding across the floor.

Poor baby. She was working out her frustrations in her play. Only what had she seen to cause such play? And when?

Daddy hitted the bad man.

Today's play had to relate to that statement, and Linney was almost certain that the scene with the dolls and stuffed animals was connected to Amy's murder. Did Drbil fit into this? Had he come for Amy? Had Dane found out and killed him? If he had—and Amy knew it—then Dane could have killed her to keep her silent.

The web was becoming much too tangled. She went into the room and sat on the floor with Julie. She didn't want to upset her, but she needed to know the name of the man Dane had attacked.

"Your bear was being mean, wasn't he?"

"No. He's good. He hitted the bad man."

"Did your Daddy tell you the man was bad?"

"Uh-huh. Mommy cried."

"Your mommy cried when your Daddy was beating up the man?"

"Uh-huh."

Linney pulled Julie into her arms and hugged her tightly. "It's okay, sweetheart. It's all going to be okay."

Julie had seen way too much for a child her age. Now she'd lost her mother, but she'd have the loving, nurturing, safe life Amy had envisioned for her. Linney would see to that, if she had to fight Dane every step of the way.

Hopefully, Dane's incarceration would prevent it from coming to that.

CUTTER LISTENED to Linney's description of her encounter with Julie on the drive to Linney's house, where he'd arranged for them to meet up with Goose. Linney's theory that Dane might have killed another man was disturbing on several levels.

But it resolved one big issue in Cutter's mind. He had no choice but to break into Dane's house and search for any incriminating evidence—the sooner the better. Dane wouldn't have lost his cool so quickly when he'd run into them at Edna Sears's home if he wasn't getting worried. He'd certainly played it differently when Linney had returned Julie to him the day before.

Today was Friday. Dane had already had seven days to destroy evidence with virtually no police interference. In fact, he may have had police help via his partner,

Wesley Evans. The two might as well have been joined at the hip, judging by how Wesley backed him up every step of the way.

Goose was a hundred percent against his searching the Colley house, but that was only because he was coming at this from a cop's vantage point. Cutter had left the room when he'd taken the phone call at Edna's to keep Linney from hearing his side of the ongoing argument about the pros and cons. But Cutter knew for sure that Goose would do the same thing in his shoes.

The shoes of a man with a woman to protect—a woman he'd go to the grave for any day of the week. He was right back where he'd said he'd never be—tangled up in Linney's seductive charms.

He could no more have kept from making love with her last night than he could have stopped the sun from coming up this morning. She was like an addiction, a drug that he knew was bad for him but that he couldn't wait to get his hands on again.

She'd walked away before, right into the lap of luxury. She'd be rich again when she had her settlement, this time living the good life with her own funds.

There was no possible way he'd fit into that life. He liked his edges rough, his days full of action, his nights looking up at starry skies.

After two months of Houston traffic snarls, white shirts and trying to find a spot in the civilian workforce, he was more certain than ever that he could never make it as a city guy. And he'd be as out of place as a horse in church if he tried to fit into Houston society.

The driver in front of him threw on his brakes and Cutter had to swerve to keep from initiating a major pileup. His stomach growled. They'd been in the car for almost an hour and were nearing the freeway exit to

Green's Harbor. "It's time for lunch," he said. "What are you hungry for?"

"I haven't thought about it."

"How about Chinese? I noticed a restaurant that looked interesting near your house yesterday."

"Dragon Delight. I've eaten there before. Food's good."

"Is that a yes?"

"Yes, but if I hang with you much longer, I'll have to exercise twice as much just to keep from losing ground."

"You planning to hang with a ranchless cowboy like me, Mrs. Kingston?" Ridiculous of him to put it on the line like that, even if he did make it sound light.

"You have a ranch—at least Merlee does. All you need to do is add cows and stir—if that's what you want." She turned to face him. "Is that what you want?"

"It might be. What about you? Do you ever think of moving back to Dobbin?"

"Why would I?"

"You could be the queen of Dobbin with the funds from your settlement."

"I have other plans for that money."

"I thought you might."

The ringing of her cell phone kept them from pursuing a conversation that was going nowhere. Linney's voice vibrated with anticipation as she answered. He knew she was hoping it was Drbil on the line.

"I told you not to call me anymore. That's why we're paying our attorneys the big bucks."

She looked at Cutter and mouthed the word *Al*.

"Yes… No… No way."

She put her hand over the phone and turned toward Cutter. "He says he has to talk to me, that the charges against him affect me as well."

A meeting with Al was fine by Cutter. In fact, it was just about perfect. He had lots of questions about Al and talking to him again might give Cutter a better feel for exactly how far the man would go to keep $4 million or more on his side of the ledger.

"Tell him we'll meet him at your place in an hour."

"What about Goose?"

"He doesn't get off duty until two."

"Al wants to see me alone."

"And I want the Texans to win the Super Bowl and the Astros to go to the World Series. Gotta learn to live with disappointment."

Al might be a multimillionaire, but he was big-time loser on lots of fronts. He'd had Linney's love and tossed it away. A man would have to be a fool to pull a stunt like that.

Cutter returned to thoughts of Linney as she told her less-than-charming ex that their meeting would be a threesome or not at all. Linney had it all. Gorgeous. Intelligent. Spunky. The courage to stand up to the whole GHPD. But none of that fully explained the way he felt about her or the dynamic combustion they created together.

She'd walk again when this was over. But at least this time he knew that going in. He'd pay later, but he knew he'd make love to her again if they spent time alone.

Hero. Man of steel. Heart of a warrior. The newspapers had written all that and more about him. Nice coverage, but Linney proved that when all was said and done, he was just a red-blooded Texas cowboy with the bad luck to fall for the wrong woman.

HE PARKED IN THE BACK ROW of the lot and watched Cutter Martin and Linney Kingston climb from the black pickup truck. The headlights on the truck blinked once as Cutter used the remote locking device.

He lifted his binoculars to his eyes and let his gaze follow them as they walked the few yards to the restaurant located at the far corner of the neighborhood strip mall. A nice-looking couple. The heroic SEAL and the attractive kindergarten teacher.

Cutter opened the glass door for Linney and put his hand on the small of her back to usher her inside. A nice, familiar touch. He imagined the two of them getting it on, her naked, straddling him. Linney would be a couple of hot handfuls.

They could have had a nice long life to enjoy each other. But Linney had refused to heed the threats. Now she'd gone too far and had to be stopped. Cutter, well, he'd just be blown along for the ride.

Hopefully, their last meal would be a good one.

Chapter Twelve

Cutter forked the last of his second spring roll and popped it into his mouth. Linney was still working on her first, though, surprisingly, her appetite had returned with the first taste.

Cutter swallowed and reached for his iced tea. "Not much I love better than Chinese food, except a good steak."

"And Merlee's famous homemade pickles. She's legendary in the county for those."

"I'll let you in on a little secret." He lowered his voice and leaned in furtively, as if they were international spies. "I always hated those." He reached for his phone. "Will you excuse me for a minute? I need to make a quick call to cancel a job interview I had scheduled for this afternoon."

"I'm sorry. I guess I've played havoc with all your plans for this week."

"Nothing big. Just a shot at another job I'd probably turn down anyway. It requires a noose around my neck from nine to five every day."

He took another long sip of his tea, then stepped outside and back into the noonday heat to make the call. Linney noticed an attractive customer at a nearby table watching him as he walked away. Who could blame her?

Cutter wore virility like a cowboy wore his Wranglers. Not ostensibly tight or stiff, just comfortably sexy. Wisps of heat curled inside her. Desire surged so easily when Cutter was around. He was a turn-on waiting to happen no matter how anxiety-filled the rest of her life.

The waitress stopped at the table to pick up Cutter's empty appetizer dish and refill his tea glass. "The entrees will be out in a few minutes."

"No hurry," Linney said. "My friend had to make a phone call." She glanced toward the window. She didn't see Cutter, but a car pulled out of the parking space in front of the restaurant, giving her a clear view of Cutter's truck.

A man walked up to the pickup while she was watching and stooped as if he were looking at the back tires.

An alarm shot through her brain. The guy could be planting a tracer on Cutter's truck the same way someone had done her car.

She dropped her fork. It clattered to the floor as she pushed away from the table and ran for the door. If she were fast enough, she could get a good look at the culprit before he did his dirty work and fled.

"Sorry," she said as she maneuvered past an elderly couple just arriving. She'd almost reached the truck when something struck her from behind, shoving her to the hard pavement.

Blood trickled from her cheek as she realized the train that had run her down was Cutter. "What are you doing? Get off me. The man's getting away."

"Run back to the restaurant, Linney. No questions. Just run!"

The order was barely out of his mouth when the explosion blasted in her ears and the ground seemed to shake beneath her. Cutter's body covered hers again as metal fragments rained from the sky, and the air crackled with bursting flames.

"You okay?" Cutter asked.

"I'm breathing."

"Then keep doing it." He jumped from atop her and started running toward the back of the parking lot. She pushed up to her elbows as a crowd gathered around her.

Someone bent over her and took her pulse. "I'm a doctor. An ambulance is on its way."

"I'm not injured, at least I don't think I am." She stood up to prove her point and to try and see Cutter. Her legs were wobbly, and her stomach was churning. And her chin felt as if someone had used sandpaper on it.

She didn't spot Cutter, but she could see Cutter's truck, or what was left of it. Half of the bed was missing.

"I'll take over from here," Cutter said. His voice rang with authority as he appeared out of nowhere and pushed his way through the bystanders. He slipped an arm around her just as a cacophony of sirens came at them from every direction.

Linney shook herself from the state of semishock. "Someone bombed your truck!"

"Looks that way."

"I tried to stop him," she said, ignoring the barrage of comments and questions flying at them from the spectators who were still huddled around them.

"I know. Thank goodness I stopped you before you got too close."

The picture was starting to clear. "He meant to kill us."

"And came damn close." Cutter pulled her into his arms. "He won't get a second chance."

"Did you see who it was?"

"No."

The crowd's clamor quieted as the police and para-medics convened on the scene. The waiting orange chicken and shrimp fried rice were forgotten in the verbal melee and confusion that followed.

Linney convinced the paramedics that her scuffed knees and scraped chin were the extent of her injuries and that she didn't need a trip in their screaming ambulance.

The police were not nearly as easy to get rid of. Cutter was close-mouthed, claiming not to have any idea why his empty truck had been targeted or why. Regardless, Linney knew that once the report got back to the GHPD, Chief Prentiss would get word of the incident.

She was sure Dane Colley was behind the explosion, either directly or by orchestrating the attempted murder from behind the scenes. She didn't know why the bomb had detonated prematurely, but she'd be eternally thankful.

She was sorry she'd pulled Cutter into this, sorry his truck was destroyed and his readjustment to civilian life disrupted. But...

"That's the second time this week you've saved my life," she whispered as the investigating cops retreated. "I owe you big time."

"Yep, you are one high-maintenance babe. But don't worry, I'm sure I can think of some way for you to repay me for the trouble."

And then he kissed her, not hungrily, as he had last night, but sweet and comforting. Confirming that even in a world where killers sometimes wore badges, heroes still rode to the rescue in jeans and a pickup truck.

THEY WERE IN A BLUE four-wheel-drive Jeep Cherokee rental, only one block from her house when Linney realized that her hands were clammy. The panic she'd felt following the explosion had settled into a jagged apprehension that ground in her stomach and rode rough-shod over her nerve endings.

She'd come within seconds and inches of being blown to bits right there in front of a neighborhood restaurant on a quiet Friday in June.

She'd barely missed being killed. Before she'd reached thirty. Before she'd married a man she could love the rest of her life. Before she'd given birth and held a precious baby of her own in her arms.

Dead before she'd really lived.

Thinking like this would reduce her to a whimpering heap of nerves if she didn't shape up. She took a deep breath and reminded Cutter to turn at the next corner.

"How much do you know about explosives?" she asked.

"Enough to know that the one that just took the back end off my new truck didn't discharge according to plan."

"How do you explain that, other than a miracle— which I'm not knocking in any way?"

"My educated guess is that the device was remotely controlled and was supposed to be detonated once we were buckled into our seats."

"What would cause it to malfunction?"

"It's likely the man who was planting it saw the pair of us running toward him, panicked and set it off either accidentally or so that he could escape in the chaos of the moment."

"Then you saw him standing behind your truck, too?"

"Not until you burst out the door. I saw him and you and…" His voice dissolved into a husky grumble. "You almost gave me a heart attack back there. I want you to promise me you won't try to be a hero again."

"Wouldn't that be a heroine? At any rate, I wasn't trying to be one. I thought he was putting a tracer on your truck so that he could kill us later."

"I don't care what you think—next time you come to me first if you suspect trouble. Only there won't be a next time. From now on, I'm not letting you out of my sight."

She liked the sound of that. "At least the explosion

gives me new evidence to take to the media. They'll have to respond now and, once they do, the police chief will be forced to have to intensify his investigation."

"I'd like you to hold off on that."

"Give me one good reason to. You were almost killed back there, too, you know."

"Let's just say I have more faith in my finding out the truth than I do Wesley Evans and his armed cohorts. Give me a chance to check out Dane's residence and for Drbil to get back to us."

"Calling him that makes him sound like a gerbil. I'm already picturing the man with rodentlike ears and small beady eyes. And speaking of rats, look who's waiting for us."

Al's red sports car was parked in her driveway. She'd forgotten all about telling him to meet them there. She glanced at her watch. "We were supposed to meet him two hours ago. He'll be livid and will demand excuses for my running so late."

"Unless he was there," Cutter said, "or sent a paid representative to the fireworks show."

"You've got to be kidding. The explosion has Dane Colley written all over it."

"I didn't see a gift card and I didn't get a good look at the perpetrator."

"It's still obvious it was him. You saw how guilty he looked at Edna's."

"Call me a doubting Thomas, but I like ironclad evidence."

"I think you just plain don't like Al and are determined to think the worst of him."

"Well, there is that."

She shook her head in exasperation and began unbuckling her seat belt.

Al was out of his car by the time Cutter killed the

engine. He struck a surly pose. "We had an appointment, and you know that I do not like to be kept waiting."

His attitude made her ditch all thought of apology or explanation. "You could have left at any time."

"Let's skip the sarcastic formalities, shall we, and just get down to business."

"Okay, start talking."

He pulled a linen handkerchief from the vest pocket of his Armani suit jacket and wiped a line of perspiration from his brow. "Let's talk inside. It's an oven out here."

"Kind of like being inside an explosion, isn't it?" Cutter said, joining them.

The comment only elicited an annoyed stare from Al. "So you're still sniffing after Linney. Too bad you returning heroes can't find something worthwhile to occupy your time."

Linney led the way to the door, unlocked it and proceeded inside and into the small family room at the rear of the house. "Don't make yourself too comfortable," she said, directing her comment at Al. "You won't be staying long."

"You're right. I've already wasted too much time waiting in your driveway. Are you sure you want the cowboy present for this discussion? It involves your personal finances."

"I'm sure I want Cutter."

Al sneered.

She took the sofa, expecting Al to take the chair. To her surprise, he sat down next to her, a little too close for comfort. She scooted over a few inches as he pulled a manila file folder from his briefcase.

"I hate to have to tell you this, but since we were married much of the period the IRS is accusing me of fraud, you're going to be part of the investigation."

"We were married, but I never owned any part of

your business. You made sure that was explicitly covered in our prenuptial agreement."

"Yes, but the fraud charges aren't limited to the business. They're saying I put personal money into a questionable tax shelter."

"You may have, but I didn't know anything about it. I had my personal checkbook with funds from my monthly allowance. That was it. Any investments you made were strictly your own doing."

"You signed the returns. I'm afraid that incriminates you. It's all here in the charges."

He pushed the file at her. She shoved it back at him and it fell to the floor, sending loose papers sailing about the room.

"What is it you want now, Al? No games, just spit it out."

"Okay. I'm in a tight spot with the Feds, Linney. I'm facing stiff penalties and fines and even that may not keep me out of jail. I don't know how all of this is going to affect the business or even if I'll be able to keep it."

"Bottom line, Al, without the whine accompaniment. I haven't heard from the Feds and I'm sure I would have if they were interested in me. So why are you really here? What kind of crooked deal do you want me to make?"

He leaned back and turned to face her. "I want to settle with you before my bank accounts are impounded by the Treasury Department."

"Great. Did you bring the check?"

"I brought a check made out to you for two million dollars. I know it's not what you want, but it's reasonable under the circumstances. My accountant has advised me against making any settlement offers until all this is behind me, but I don't want you to end up with nothing."

Cutter stood and walked over to stand in front of Al. "What's reasonable is what you agreed to in the prenuptial contract."

Al shot Cutter a go-to-hell look. "This is none of your business."

"You're right. If it were, I'd have kicked your butt out the door about a dozen pathetic lies ago. Do you think his offer is reasonable, Linney?"

"Sounds like hogwash to me."

"Guess that means you can take your paltry check and crawl back in your hole," Cutter said.

Al's face twisted into a mask of rage. He jumped to his feet, reared back and took a swing at Cutter. Cutter blocked the blow with his left fist and slammed his right fist into Al's jaw as Linney scrambled to dodge the flying punches.

Al stumbled backward, falling against the sofa only to come up again swinging. Cutter delivered a left jab that sent Al spinning to the floor.

"That one was for me," Cutter said as Al struggled back to his feet. "This one's for Linney." He slammed Al again, this time making a gusher of his nose. "And if you or any of your hired goons ever lay a hand on Linney again, or hurt her in any way, you'll have to pay a plastic surgeon to pull that sneer of yours out of your tonsils."

"You'll pay for this, you son of a bitch."

Al's threatening insult didn't carry much of a sting, since he was holding the handkerchief to his bloody nose and backing away as fast as his shaky legs would carry him.

Linney was awed, not only by the exhibition of Cutter's impressive, masculine strength, but because it had all been for her benefit. He'd defended her rights and her honor. No man had ever done that before, at least not so forcibly.

The door slammed as Al let himself out.

"I'm sorry," Cutter said.

"Why? You were awesome."

"I'd just had all I could take today. Once he swung at me, I switched to autopilot."

"Al works out five days a week. He thinks he's tougher than reinforced steel. You may have broken his nose but you most definitely devastated his pride." She rose to her tiptoes and put her arms around his neck. "If I had a purple heart, I'd pin it on you."

"Guess I'll just have to settle for a kiss."

Tears burned at the back of her lids as she melted into the sweet touch of his lips on hers and the heated mingling of their breaths. Her life was trapped in a smoldering pit of murder, threats and danger, and there was no indication that she would escape from it anytime soon.

Under those circumstances, it made utterly no sense that she could thrill to Cutter's lips on hers, but her heart didn't seem to get that message.

GOOSE KICKED OUT of a pair of tan boat shoes and propped his feet up on her coffee table. A hole in the dark blue sock on his right foot let his big toe wiggle through. The man had taken her offer to make himself at home seriously. She liked that about him.

"I wouldn't worry about Cutter if I were you, Linney. The man's got a sixth sense about danger. He smells it before anyone else sees it coming."

But she *was* worried, along with agitated that Cutter wouldn't let her go with him to Dane's. "He's breaking the law by going into Dane's house, even if he does have the key that Amy gave me."

Goose tipped back his head and downed a generous gulp of beer, the second of the six-pack he'd brought with him. His Adam's apple nodded its consent to the cold brew.

"Technically, he's only bending the law," Goose said. "And if he finds evidence in the Colley house, it's only because the GHPD hasn't done its job."

"If he finds evidence by breaking in, will it be admissible in court?"

"It all depends," Goose said. "He's not there in an official capacity. He's just a friend of a friend with a key. But I think what he's looking for is a clue as to what really went on at the Colley home last Friday morning."

"I'm not sure what he could possibly find except Amy's laptop."

"If there was a fight there with another man as the kid's words and actions suggested, he could find evidence of that."

"I guess. I'd hoped we'd hear from Amy's mystery e-mail buddy by now, but no luck with that."

"Give him time."

"I don't understand why Cutter didn't ask you to go with him," she said. "I know I'd feel better if he had backup."

"I'm a cop. As long as I wear the badge I have to follow the rules. That's the thing with being a cop. I like what I do, but all the restrictions seem designed to give the perp the edge."

"You sound like Cutter now. He has a monumental disdain for rules."

"For rules that serve no good purpose. Anyway, Cutter didn't need or want me in on this. He's in his element, and this is a one-man operation."

"So he told me." More than once. "You and Cutter must be very good friends."

"Close as brothers. Well, closer in my case. We met right after he got his first assignment. Even as a green rookie, he was a hell of a fighter. We were on the same team for countless operations after that, lots of them behind enemy lines when all we had to count on was each other. Men bond fast in those situations."

"Were you there when he got shot?"

"I was. His actions that day are the reason I'm alive now."

"Were you injured, too?"

"I broke my arm in a fall off a cliff during the first stages of the attack."

"Is that why you left the service?"

"No. I'd finished three tours of duty, and I was pushing thirty-four. I figured it was time I came home and tried to give my wife the kids she wanted."

"Cutter never mentioned that you were married."

"I'm not. Susie presented me with divorce papers soon after I hit the home front. Seemed she'd gotten along without me too well."

"Ouch."

"I said a little worse than that, but I'm over it now. Military life is hard on marriage."

"I guess that's why Cutter never tried it."

"That and the fact that he'd had his heart broken by some woman before he made full SEAL."

"I didn't know." And now that she did, she wished she didn't. She wondered where their five days in San Diego fit into that picture.

Had she been his rebound affair? Or had he met someone after their tryst? "What was she like? Did he say?"

"Not really, and guys don't ask questions about things like that. All I know is she was a heartbreak waiting to happen. They had a whirlwind romance and then she blew him off for some bastard with money to burn. He was lucky he didn't tie the knot with a woman like that."

A whirlwind romance. Like five electrifying days and just as many torrid nights of making love. Could *she* possibly the heartbreaker Goose was referring to?

Impossible. They'd made love as if they were the only two people in the world, but all Cutter had talked about was his future as a SEAL. Even the passion had seemed intertwined with his excitement over becoming a naval commando.

He'd never indicated that he wanted anything more than a fling with her and he'd never tried to get in touch with her again. But if there was even a chance that he'd had real feelings for her and had spoken about her to Goose, she wanted to get to the bottom of it.

Goose finished his beer. "Mind if I turn on the TV? There's an afternoon news show on one of the military-friendly cable stations I catch when I can."

"Go for it." She tossed him the remote, thankful to be relieved of making further conversation. Her mind was bogged down with more pressing matters.

Like Cutter's getting in and out of Dane's house without detection. And if it was possible that he'd ever kidded himself into believing that she was the reason they'd never followed up on their affair.

CUTTER WAS TENSE, racked with apprehension and the murderous questions that clashed like cymbals in his mind. None of his fears had anything to do with breaking into the Colley home. Action was the easy part of all this.

The fear came from knowing someone would go to any extreme to silence Linney. He'd have a lot better grasp on Dane's possible involvement in that if he could find one solid piece of evidence today to prove the murder theory.

He was about to get that chance. Dane was nowhere

around. Cutter had snooped enough to be certain of that. And no one had seen Cutter approach the house from the back or watched him slip into the thin, supple latex gloves that would keep him from leaving prints without affecting his dexterity.

Skulking toward the back of the garage, he squeezed through the small window over Dane's worktable. The key Linney had given him was in his front pocket, but it was to the front door, in plain sight of the neighbors, if any were looking.

The garage window was hidden from view by a thick row of shrubbery and the privacy fence around the pool.

He moved quickly and silently, as he'd done on countless reconnaissance operations. The terrain and the circumstances were vastly different here, but his skill and training served him just as well.

He had that same rush of adrenaline, a spike in all his senses, a single-mindedness of purpose that ratcheted every brain cell into high gear.

He'd missed this feeling every day since leaving the SEALs. Only he'd never wanted to find it again because Linney was in danger.

He slipped through the garage and into the house through an unlocked back door. He searched room by room, looking for anything that might offer a clue. A patch of carpet in the master bedroom appeared to have been cleaned recently. If it was due to blood from a fight with another man at the time of the murder, the investigation could likely still detect it, though the DNA might be questionable.

Most of the house was neat and spotlessly clean. By contrast, makeup items were scattered about Amy's dressing table. It looked as if she'd been putting on her face when something—or someone—interrupted her.

Had she heard something in the pool area that she'd run to investigate? Had that been how Dane had lured her out there on a hot summer morning?

Dane or someone else? He hated to stress the point around Linney, but even if she'd been murdered, Amy's background left the field wide open for possible suspects.

Cutter paused at the display of framed photographs crowded across the top of a bookshelf. Most were of Julie, with and without Amy and Dane. Some were of Amy and Dane or of the two of them and Wesley. A few were just of Amy and Wesley or of Dane and Wesley.

Detective Evans had clearly been a big part of their private life. They might have been close enough that Wesley helped him plan the whole thing, thinking that between the two of them they could definitely get away with murder.

They would have—if Linney hadn't foiled their plans. It was just a theory at this point, but it made sense. Unfortunately, there was no sign of Amy's laptop or any letters, notes or a journal.

Cutter slipped back into the garage.

He perused the area quickly. A late-model Toyota Highlander, which he assumed had been Amy's car, was parked on the left. Julie's booster seat was in the backseat along with a McDonald's wrapper that had fallen to the floor behind the driver's seat.

The compartment between the front seats held a padded case full of CDs, a pen, a tube of hand cream and a gasoline receipt dated the Thursday before she'd died. That didn't prove a thing, but it did make sense to have the car full of gas if she'd been planning on leaving the next morning. He slipped the receipt into his pocket.

The glove compartment held the usual—car manuals and an envelope with insurance and registration information. Cutter pulled them out just to make sure he hadn't missed anything. His fingers brushed cold hard metal. Pushing further, he grasped the butt of a pistol.

He grabbed his cell phone and made a quick photograph of the gun still in place. Then he pulled it out for a better look. A small, black .38. He copied the seven-digit ID number in his notebook, then put everything back as he'd found it.

It would be interesting to see if the weapon was registered in Amy's name and, if so, when she'd purchased it.

That was all the exploration of the garage produced. He was about to climb back onto the worktable and let himself out the same way he'd come in when something caught his eye. It was lodged in the slant of space between the top of a tool rack and the bottom of the window facing. A small square printed with the letter *F.* A key from a computer keyboard.

A grinding sound above him and the flash of overhead illumination snapped him back to the risks at hand. Someone had pulled into the driveway and the garage door was inching upward.

Chapter Thirteen

Instinctively, the palm of Cutter's right hand grazed the pistol resting in his shoulder holster as he reached for the screwdriver at the back of the worktable. With a flick of his wrist he snapped the *F* key loose from its hiding place. It toppled onto the table along with a fragment of hard white plastic.

Cutter pushed against the table, trapping the plastic keyboard piece between his stomach and the edge of the worktable. He picked up both of the pieces he'd dislodged. The one without a letter on it was squashed almost flat.

The door was fully raised and the car was creeping inside the garage when Cutter jumped to the tabletop and through the open window.

There was a chance Dane hadn't noticed his escape since the table was in a rectangular work area that extended beyond the Highlander. Hoping for the best, Cutter took a split second to push the screen back into place. A second later he scaled the shrubbery and raced toward the wooded green area just beyond the back of the row of houses.

He didn't hear yells, gunfire or the tramp of running feet, so he slowed to a nonchalant walk as he neared the rental car he'd left parked on a neighboring street. Once he was inside his car with the engine running, he dug the *F* key and the chip of plastic from his pocket.

He continued to stare at the chip, rolling it between his thumb and index finger as drove away. The pattern looked familiar.

Finally he realized why. The plastic was a smashed version of the emblem on the front of his laptop. A loose key and a pounded emblem from a notebook computer. As far as Cutter was concerned, the mystery of what had happened to Amy's computer was solved. Dane had destroyed it.

It looked more and more as if Dane had killed his wife, but there was still no clear-cut evidence to prove his guilt. And, unfortunately, Cutter was afraid that Dane was too integral a member of the homicide department's family for them to work hard at proving him guilty.

Which left finding the truth up to Cutter. The real challenge was finding it before a desperate madman succeeded in silencing Linney forever.

LINNEY WAS THRILLED with the evidence Cutter had found and more elated that he hadn't been shot in an exchange of gunfire with Dane Colley. Even Goose was impressed with the *F* key and the battered, but still recognizable trademark emblem.

Goose stretched his arms and yawned.

"You tired, boy?" Cutter barked. "Give me thirty."

Linney jumped out of the way as both men hit the floor and started doing pushups. It was a glistening display of perspiration and muscle and the nicest pair of butts she'd ever seen. And she had no idea what any of it was about.

"I would have joined you," she quipped when they finished and stood to give each other high fives. "But I figured this was some kind of private SEAL bonding ritual."

"Something like that," Goose agreed, "but feel free to jump in any time. We'll stop and watch you flex."

"I'll just bet you would."

"So what are you going to do next?" Goose asked.

"No plans except to drive back to the ranch, get some rest and hope we hear from Drbil."

"We could stay here tonight," Linney offered. "It's a long drive to Dobbin."

"You got that right," Goose said. "It's thirty minutes back to Houston in light traffic and Dobbin has to be another hour and a half."

"Close," Cutter agreed, "but I think better at the ranch. I hadn't realized how suffocating and stifling my stint in city life had been until I got back to the Double M the other night.

"Beside it's easier to protect Linney out there. The area around the house is wide open. It would be impossible for someone to sneak right up to the house without being noticed."

"Unless you're asleep," Goose noted.

"I never sleep so soundly that I can't hear footsteps where they have no business being. And there aren't neighbors milling around the Double M or driving by for that matter."

Goose grinned. "It sounds as if you may be leaning toward going back into ranching."

"I like the atmosphere. I'm not sure tending cows will do it for me."

"Go into law enforcement. I'm sure the sheriff's office out there could use someone like you."

Cutter shook his head. "Then I'd have to deal with all those rules, the bureaucracy and those political games you're always griping about."

"It might not be that bad outside the city."

"Then again, it might be worse," Cutter said. "I'd know the people I was arresting. I'm not knocking what you do. I'm just not feeling the pull to do it myself."

Goose slipped his feet back into his shoes. "I've got to get out of here if I'm going to drop Edna's computer off at George Billinger's for you. He said it would be tomorrow before he can get started on it, but he's the best man around for the job. He was an expert with the FBI before he retired and started his own computer forensics consulting business."

"Sounds like just the man we need."

"Yeah, buddy, and I can give you the name of some good bodyguards if you want some backup at the Double M."

"I can handle the job myself."

Goose gave him a friendly punch. "I expect you can. And if you find that you can't, I can always take Linney off your hands for you."

Cutter didn't take him up on the offer, but he didn't actually refuse it, either. Goose said his good-byes and she waited in the kitchen while Cutter walked him to the door.

She was glad there would be no backup tonight. She wanted the chance to be alone with Cutter back at the ranch. They'd danced around the five days in San Diego long enough. They needed to bring the past out into the open.

But it wasn't just past history that she needed clarified. It was his present feelings as well. She loved making love to him, but she needed more than just a whirlwind of passion that Cutter would toss aside when he went on with his life again.

Six years had changed her, too. She'd only just begun to realize how much.

THEY WERE ABOUT HALFWAY BACK to Dobbin when Linney received a phone call from a frantic Edna Sears.

"Dane just called me. His voice was slurred and I'm certain he's drunk."

"What did he want?" Linney asked.

"He's coming for Julie. He cursed me out on the phone, said I was a traitor to my own daughter for cooperating with you. I've never heard him sound so angry. It's just not like him."

So Edna was finally seeing the side of Dane that Amy must have seen many times. A cold dread settled in Linney's chest.

"He shouldn't be minding Julie when he's drunk and angry."

"I know," Edna said. "I pleaded with him not to come. I told him I wouldn't let him take Julie with him when he was drinking, but I'm afraid he may show up anyway."

"Go to Cutter's ranch in Dobbin with us. We're in your area now. We can pick you up," Linney said, blurting out the invitation without even thinking to ask Cutter first.

"I don't know. Dane will be furious if he finds out I left here with you."

"Does that matter as much as keeping Julie safe?"

"No, but…what if he doesn't let me see her again? I love her so much, and she's all I have left of Amy."

If there was any justice, Dane would be in prison and Edna would have full custody of her granddaughter. But in this case justice wasn't only blind, but absent altogether.

"Dane will cool down when he sobers up and be glad Julie didn't see him in an angry, drunken state," Linney reasoned. "And even if he doesn't understand, you have to put Julie's welfare first."

"You're right. It's just that I'm so rattled I can barely think."

"Don't think. Just pack an overnight bag for you and Julie. We'll be there in…" She glanced at Cutter and knew from the grim pull to his lips that he'd gotten the drift of the conversation.

"Under fifteen minutes," he said.

She relayed the information to Edna then broke the connection so that Edna could make the necessary preparations.

"I invited them to your place without asking," Linney said. "I hope that's okay."

"It was the only responsible thing you could do."

"You didn't feel that way the other night when I showed up at your condo with Julie."

"Kidnapping a little girl to get media attention is far different from a grandmother protecting her grandchild from an angry, drunken father."

Not to mention the fact that the father was an abusive, murdering, dirty cop who'd tried to blow Linney and Cutter to smithereens just hours earlier.

Having Edna and Julie at the ranch would likely mean she wouldn't get to have her long-overdue confrontation with Cutter tonight, but that had waited six years. Another night wouldn't make that much difference.

Still, when his hand rode the back of the seat and curled around her shoulder, tingles of heated anticipation skipped through her. Whatever else existed between them, whatever might happen in the future, the raw, wild, unadulterated passion would haunt her memories for the rest of her life.

DUSK WAS A SOOTHING, magical time at the ranch. A gentle breeze whispered through the trees. The high-pitched chorus of tree frogs and crickets was interrupted only by the neighing of horses and the croak of a bullfrog in the nearby creek.

Julie was running around the front yard of the sprawling, two-story ranch house, chasing the dozens of darting fireflies that made the lawn a glittering fairyland. She'd had lots of questions at first about why they were spending the night at the ranch again, but she seemed perfectly at ease now.

Linney and Edna were sitting in the porch swing sipping glasses of a fruity red wine. Cutter was perched on the banister at the other end of the porch, staring into space and nursing a cup of strong, hot coffee. She knew he wanted his senses glaringly clear in case Dane brought his anger or danger out to Dobbin.

Edna dabbed at her eyes with a crumpled tissue. "I can't think of Amy without crying. Realizing that Dane may have killed her makes her death so much worse. That may not make sense, but it's true."

"It makes sense to me."

"She never told me she was afraid of him. You'd think she would have."

"I'm sure she didn't want to upset you or bring you into the mess."

"No, it's because I let her down before. I didn't approve of the way she lived her life. I was mortified that she'd become an addict and that she'd used her body in such depraved ways."

"That was all behind her."

"That doesn't change the fact that I let her down. She called me once when she was living in Los Angeles. She begged me to come out for a visit. I refused to go."

"She must have forgiven you. She came back to Texas and settled in the Houston area so that she could be near you."

"I guess you're right. When she told me she was pregnant with a little girl, she said she wanted me to be part of her daughter's life and that she'd never do anything to shame me again. She just wanted to be a good mother."

"Were she and Dane married when she got pregnant?"

"No, but they got married shortly after that. They didn't have a church wedding or anything. They just came by one afternoon and told me they'd been to a justice of the peace."

"And she seemed happy about the marriage?"

"Very happy. And Dane was charming. I remember thinking how much in love he seemed. He literally couldn't keep his hands or his eyes off her."

Linney hated to pry, but she needed to know the truth. "Did Amy seem to be in love with Dane?"

Edna pushed the short strands of graying hair back from her face and then dabbed her eyes again. "She wasn't as adoring as he was, but that's not her way."

So the answer was no. Yet Edna hadn't questioned that the baby might not be Dane's, not even at this point, when she suspected he'd killed Amy.

But if Dane had any suspicions that Julie might not have been his, he would have surely had DNA testing done before now.

Julie ran onto the porch. "I catched one, Grandma. See his light." She opened her cupped hands for Edna and then Linney to peer inside. When she'd collected their awes, she ran to Cutter. After he'd seen it, she opened her hands and let the firefly loose.

"He wants to go home," she said.

"His home is right here on the ranch," Cutter said. "He has lots of room here to flap his wings and acres of space to explore."

Linney wondered if he were talking about the insect or about himself. The ranch suited his rugged ways. And it wasn't just that he looked smoking-hot in worn jeans, scuffed boots and his Western hat. He looked like a simple cowboy, but he was a complex man with the heart of a warrior.

He'd battled and defeated some of the world's most aggressive fighters. She didn't see how ranching could ever satisfy his need for danger and adventure.

Which left her exactly where she'd been six years ago. She could turn him on but she couldn't hold on to him.

She needed another glass of wine. She excused herself and went back to the kitchen. Her glass was half-full when her phone rang.

The jangle startled her. She checked the caller ID. William Gibbons. She didn't recognize the name or the area code. She answered it anyway.

"Hello?"

"This is Dr. Bill Gibbons. I was asked to call someone at this number."

Dr. Bill. Drbil. Her mouth went dry. "Are you calling in response to my e-mail concerning Amy Colley?"

"I am. Is there a problem? Is Amy okay?"

"No. She's dead."

The line went silent for so long Linney thought the doctor might have hung up.

"When did this happen?"

"Last Friday. She drowned in her home pool."

"That rotten, degenerate son of a bitch."

"The drowning was ruled an accident."

"It was no accident. Dane Colley killed her." His voice was hoarse and shaky. "I knew it was only a matter of time. What about her daughter? Is Julie okay?"

"As well as can be expected. She misses her mother, though I don't think she really understands yet that she won't be coming back."

"Dead," he said again, as if he couldn't get past the shock and pain.

"Dr. Gibbons, it's critical that you tell me whatever you can about Amy and Dane's relationship."

"Are you with the police?"

"No, I'm just a friend of Amy's."

"Linney?"

"Yes. I guess I should have given my name when I wrote you."

"It would have helped. Amy's mentioned you. She considered you a trusted friend."

"I was very fond of Amy, too, and I agree with you that Dane killed her. The problem is that the truth is a tough sell to the Green's Harbor Police Department, what with Dane being a homicide detective. That's why I'm hoping you can help."

The silence set in again. "I'd rather not talk about this on the phone." His voice dissolved into a shuddering sob.

"I can come wherever you are."

"I'm in the Baltimore area, but I'll come there. I should be able to get a flight to Houston in the morning."

"That would be great. My friend Cutter and I can meet you at the airport. Just call me back when you have your flight information."

"Yes. Be careful, Linney. Dane is a depraved man. I wouldn't put anything past him."

"I'm being careful," she assured him. She would be dead herself if Cutter hadn't saved her life twice.

She hated that she'd have to wait a few more hours to hear what Dr. Gibbons had to say, but at least his answers would be forthcoming and, hopefully, they'd be enough to put Dane behind bars for the next sixty years or so.

"WESLEY, DO YOU HAVE A MINUTE? I'd like to talk to you about Amy Colley's drowning."

Wesley unwittingly ground his teeth as he stopped making his way to the elevator and turned back to face the chief. The dark patch of five o'clock shadow gave Saul's ruddy face an almost comical look. Not that Saul was smiling.

"My office," Saul said.

Wesley turned and followed the man through the scramble of chairs and desks in the booking room and past the crowded cubicles that served as offices for the detectives. Dane's cubicle was empty. He'd left mid-afternoon in a mood that bordered on morose.

Wesley suspected that his partner was drunk and passed out at home in his own recliner by now. But that wouldn't be what this meeting was about. Saul had told Dane to take as much time as he needed to deal with Amy's death. It had been Dane's decision to come back to work so soon.

"Take a seat," Saul said.

Wesley moved the day's newspaper and a used coffee cup from the chair nearest Saul's cluttered desk to the window ledge. He dropped into the seat. "What's up?"

"Did you hear about the explosion in front of the Chinese restaurant at Water's Edge Mall this afternoon?"

"I heard."

"Then I guess you also heard that it was Cutter Martin's truck that was blown up."

"Yep."

"Linney Kingston was with him."

"That was no surprise. The two are tighter than fries in a lunch special."

"You know that this means I have to reopen the case of Amy's drowning."

Wesley shrugged. "Cutter's a war hero. The guy who planted the explosive was probably one of those antiwar nuts trying to make a point and get his name in the paper."

"That's possible, but I can't ignore the fact that it could be related to Linney's suspicions about Dane, especially after she claims someone tried to shoot her from a passing car earlier this week."

"What about Dane's alibi?"

"His alibi for the shooting attempt will hold up, but his alibi for Amy's death was never as ironclad as we said. You know that. No one would pay much attention if one of the instructors took an extra-long coffee or bathroom break. Not when there were three guys teaching the class."

Wesley had expected it might come to this from the second Linney stuck her nose into the case. "This isn't going to go down well with Dane. The guy's still grieving."

"I realize that. I don't have a lot of choice. I answer to the mayor and the town's citizens. I'm going to call Dane in for questioning and then I'm going to suspend him with pay until we can get to the bottom of this."

"He'll see the suspension as kicking him when he's down," Wesley said, knowing it was true. "Dane loves his job."

"I realize that," Saul said. "I hate to do it to him. He's a damn good homicide detective."

"Guess you should tell him that," Wesley said.

"I will, and hopefully we can clear up everything quickly. I thought I should let you know about my decision since you've been helping me with the investigation."

"I didn't have a lot of choice in the matter. You're the boss."

"Some days I wish I wasn't."

Wesley frowned. "Am I supposed to alert Dane that this is going down? If I am, I'm not crazy about taking on that task."

"No. This was just for your information." Saul stood and walked to the front of his desk. "Off the record, do you think he could have killed her?"

"Off the record?"

"Just between the two of us."

Wesley shifted in his chair while he considered his words. "He's my partner. I don't want to think he could have done it."

"But I'm getting the impression that you do."

"He's got a temper. If she was really leaving him, the way Linney claims, I guess…" He stopped and shook his head. "No. I don't think he could have killed her. Not intentionally. Not unless…"

"Not unless he snapped. I got you," Saul said. "I'm hoping he's innocent and that this never goes to trial. But you know what they say about hope."

Wesley nodded. He felt like a stinking traitor. Dane didn't deserve this. He had his problems, but he was a hell of a detective. Too bad it had come to this.

But Wesley knew what he had to do.

CUTTER LEANED AGAINST THE COLUMN at the edge of the front steps and watched a streak of lightning dance across the sky. The heavens had become a backdrop for a dazzling display of electric current over the last half hour.

Thunderstorms could appear from nowhere this time of the year and were frequently intense, with gusty wind, booming thunder and rain falling in sheets. Normally he enjoyed a good storm. It cleaned the pollen from the air and left behind a sense of calm, like making up after a fight.

There would be no sense of calm tonight. Even after the storm's fury had dissipated, the tempest inside him would persist. Oddly, it wasn't from the danger or the dilemma of whether or not Dane Colley had killed his wife and had orchestrated the attempts on Linney's life.

His spirit fed on risk and mental quandary the way some men thrived on sports or chasing women. He'd been tutored in facing the worst life could hurl at you and never giving up. The concept of failure didn't exist in the SEAL philosophy, and he'd been a frogman right down to his gut.

He still was, in his mind and in his heart. That's what made adjusting to a world without danger and constant challenges so difficult. It was why protecting Linney and finding justice for little Julie's mother made him feel alive again. It was why he absolutely could not fail them.

The tempest roaring inside was all about his feelings for Linney. He'd nursed his grudge against her for years, spent immeasurable emotional energy convincing himself that she was a manipulating gold digger with no heart.

After all, she'd spent five glorious days and nights with him only to get up on the last morning and just walk away.

They'd been great together, but she'd married money. And now she'd have her settlement to ensure that she'd land on top. Not that Cutter had anything against being rich, in theory. But the lifestyle would never suit him.

It would be hell all over again to fall for her and then lose her. But he'd already fallen, and right now the need to hold her and make love with her was pulsating through him like the current zigzagging across the sky.

He went back inside the house as the first raindrops pelted the roof. He passed the door to the master suite and heard Edna's clattering snore and Julie's soft, rhythmic breathing. A gentle glow escaped from beneath Linney's door. The lamp was still on.

He paused for only a second before tapping softly. "Linney." His voice sounded thick, as if it had been filtered through cotton.

"Come in."

She was wearing the same black pajamas that he'd torn from her gorgeous body last night. His heart pumped like crazy. The blood rushed to his head. His body grew painfully hard.

"What is it, Cutter?"

"I just wanted to…" To ravage her. To give in to the erotic passions that were pushing him over the edge. "To make sure you're okay."

"I'm fine. I just can't sleep. Is it raining yet?"

"Just started." Small talk when the need inside him was raging so intensely he could barely breathe.

He gave up and crossed the room, sliding into the bed beside her and pulling her into his arms. She melted into his kiss and the thrill of her rode through him in hot waves. He slipped his hand beneath the pajama top, the cool satiny fabric caressing the back of his hands while his fingers trailed her flesh.

He kissed her again, hungrily, as his hands cupped her perfect breasts. But when his lips left her mouth, she pulled away.

"I can't do this, Cutter."

The rejection stung as if she'd slapped him. He started to slide from the bed, but she grabbed his arm and held on so tightly that her fingertips dug into his flesh.

"We need to talk."

The four words men dreaded most from a woman. It always meant you weren't measuring up. He exhaled slowly. "Okay, you start."

"Who broke your heart and turned you against women, Cutter? Who did you love and lose?"

Chapter Fourteen

"What did Goose tell you?"

Linney's heart sank and her determination faltered. She had no right to demand answers of Cutter. Making love with him didn't mean she was entitled to stake a claim. Yet she couldn't give herself so completely to him again without knowing if a relationship with him had a chance of working.

"Goose mentioned that a woman in your past had broken your heart and left you so bitter you'd never given love with anyone else a chance."

"Goose talks too much."

"He spoke as if it were common knowledge."

"In the first place, I'm not bitter. I'm just not prone to jump into relationships."

"Just into bed."

"So that's what this is about? You think I took last night too lightly."

"I just need to know one thing, Cutter. Was your heart broken before or after we hooked up in San Diego?"

Cutter left the bed and walked to the window, drawing the curtains and opening the blinds. Raindrops splattered the windowpanes and trickled off in cascading streams.

"Why is this so important to you?" he asked, his gaze still fixed on the blackness outside.

"I need to know where I fit into the picture. Was I the rebound girl? Did all that passion and fire we shared actually have anything to do with me or was it just that I was there?"

Asking the question hurt. The answer might hurt a lot more. She'd accepted years ago that she could never compete with the excitement of being a SEAL. Before Goose's pronouncement, she'd never even considered that it was another woman she'd lost out to.

"You're the one who walked out without saying good-bye, Linney."

"I hate good-byes. And that's all it would have been. I cry and you pat me on the head and try to hide your excitement at going off to finish your training and accept your assignment. You couldn't wait to move on to the next post."

"And you hurried off to marry Al Kingston. What was it, two months later? Glad you didn't squander any tears on our good-byes. What a waste that would have been."

The resentment in his voice set off a cacophony of dissonant chords. Her marriage to Al had been a mistake—she knew that better than anyone. But it had nothing to do with what had happened between her and Cutter. If it did, it was just that she'd never expected anyone to compare with him.

She kicked her feet over the side of the bed and padded across the floor to stand beside him. "You want to know the truth about my relationship with Al? Fine. He'd asked me to marry him before I ran into you in San Diego."

The bare facts sounded sordid, but if she expected the truth from Cutter, then she had to deliver it herself. Besides, there were already too many secrets and half-truths between them. If there was a chance for them, they had to change that.

"You never mentioned that you were engaged."

"I wasn't. I hadn't given him an answer. My friends all thought I was a fool not to jump at the chance to marry a man like Al, but I wasn't in love with him. Not then." Probably not ever, though God knew she'd tried to convince herself that she was.

"Making love with me must have convinced you what a great catch Al was."

"Do you want to hear this or not?"

Finally, he turned and faced her. His dark eyes seemed distant and cold, as if he'd closed himself off from her. "I'm sorry, Linney. Speak your piece. Tell me about how Al Kingston and his money swept you off your feet."

"We met in Houston. I was a paid worker for the governor's reelection campaign and was serving barbecue at one of the thousand-dollar-a-plate fund-raisers. Al was one of the contributors in attendance."

"Good old Al."

"Anyway, he was with a striking brunette that night who seemed to know everyone at the affair. I thought they were married when he struck up a conversation with me and told me I should give him a call and talk to him about a job in his store. He said he paid a lot better than the governor."

"Nothing wrong with a woman making a living."

His scorn was difficult to take, but she had to get through this. "I never took the job. We started dating and he began plying me with flowers and jewelry and taking me to expensive restaurants and fancy parties. I was awed. You have to remember that I didn't grow up the way you did. My family didn't own a huge ranch. My dad was an alcoholic who seldom kept a job for more than a few months at a time. My mother cleaned houses to pay the bills and buy groceries."

"I didn't realize—"

She put up a hand to hush him. "I'm not looking for your sympathy, Cutter. I'm just trying to make you see how it was for me. And, yes, if I'm totally honest, being with you those five days in San Diego did make it easier for me to marry Al. What you and I shared was fireworks and nonstop passion. It was fantasy, the proverbial castle in the sky where the prince fulfills every dream."

She swallowed hard. It was love. She just hadn't known it then. "I went back to Al and he convinced me that what I shared with him was the real thing. We had fun. We laughed. I'd never have to worry about bills. And I wanted kids—lots of them. I still do."

"So you walked away from me for security and wealth. I get it, Linney. And when you get that settlement that you're so determined to acquire, you'll have both. Looks like you made the right decision after all."

The sarcasm cut through her like a rapier, delivering the truth with the pain. She was the one Goose had been talking about, the woman who'd supposedly broken Cutter's heart. He'd blamed her for six long years and the past was still festering inside him.

"I don't know what you told yourself about what happened between us, Cutter Jackson Martin, but maybe I'd just better remind you of how it really was."

"I don't need any reminders."

"I think you do. We were dynamite together, but you never once said that. You didn't say you loved me or that you couldn't live without me or even that you'd keep in touch. You were high on becoming a SEAL and all the adventure that entailed. I may have been the one who walked away, but you were never really there."

She turned away. Tears were burning at the back of

her eyes and her insides were shaking. "I was crazy about you from the time I was twelve years old, Cutter. The five days we spent together were a dream. But a woman can't live on dreams."

He reached for her. She backed away. "I appreciate what you've done the last few days, Cutter, I really do. But I just can't deal with any more right now. I can't deal with us. Please, just go."

He nodded. That's all, just a nod as if they'd had a conversation about the storm and the discussion was finished. She threw herself across the bed as the door closed behind him. The tears fell like the blinding rain outside the window.

She cried for the passion they'd shared those five days in San Diego that she'd never know again. She cried for herself because she'd never feel Cutter's arms around her again.

Mostly she cried because her heart hurt and because the tears just wouldn't stop coming.

CUTTER SPENT THE NIGHT trying to do what he'd done on hundreds of other lonely nights. He forced his focus to the operation at hand. Only this time he couldn't shake Linney or her accusations from his consciousness.

They'd stung when she hurled them at him. Aunt Merlee always said that truth could be the most bitter of pills. This one was still clogged in his throat.

He had been eating, sleeping and breathing SEALs those heady days six years before. He'd just finished his BUD/S training, a feat that only 17 percent of his starting group had accomplished. He was certain he'd talked about it constantly, probably bragged about his success. He'd been on top of the friggin' world.

And then along came Linney. Sexy. Sweet. Daring.

A breath of fresh air after weeks of sweat, sand and physical exhaustion. His prize for endurance.

So maybe he had taken falling in love for granted. Maybe he hadn't been in a position to talk about marriage and kids the way Al had. Had he been, there was no guarantee it would have made a difference.

Al offered luxury—in marriage and in divorce. Cutter never would. For the good of his country, he'd rounded up risks and danger, instead of cattle. But he was still just a cowboy at heart.

At sunup, he put in a call to Goose and got the name of a bodyguard. By nine o'clock, they'd finished breakfast and were in the rental car, on their way to meet the doctor and hopefully bring the Dane Colley arrest operation to a grand finale.

They all needed closure in the worst way.

AMY'S DEAD. Amy's dead. Amy's dead.

The words echoed in Bill Gibbons's mind, over and over, every repetition a knife slicing away a sliver of his heart. The flight from Baltimore to Houston seemed to go on forever. Each second of it felt like pure torture.

This was all his fault. He should have gone to the police. No. Dane *was* the police. He should have gotten a gun and put a bullet through Dane Colley's brain. If he'd shot him last Friday, Amy would still be alive.

Bill wasn't a violent man. He'd never even been in a real fight until last week. Then he'd been no match for Dane. The detective's fists had plowed into his ribs like a club, splintering bone and making pulp of his tissue.

He would give Linney the information she wanted. She thought that would bring Amy justice. He wasn't convinced. That's why he knew what he'd have to do.

He was going to kill Dane Colley.

"Please return all tray tables to their upright position and return you personal belongings to their original stored locations. Prepare for landing."

For once in his life, Bill was fully prepared.

WHEN THEY'D BROUGHT Edna and her granddaughter home, they'd waited at the Sears home until the body-guard Cutter had hired arrived. Edna had been alarmed that he thought protection was necessary in the bright light of day. "Just to be on the safe side," he'd assured her.

Dr. Gibbons's flight was scheduled to arrive at 11:00 a.m. Even after waiting for the bodyguard, Linney and Cutter had arrived at the airport with time to spare. Things had been strained between them all morning, and standing idly in the clusters of strangers wasn't helping matters.

Cutter sauntered back after checking the nearby arrivals display screen. "His plane is at the gate."

"I should have asked what he looked like or how he'd be dressed," she said, suddenly nervous and apprehensive that this wasn't going to be the turning point she was hoping for.

"He'll see our sign."

Linney stared at the hand-printed sign Cutter was holding up. Dr. William Gibbons. She didn't even know what kind of doctor he was or how his life had become entangled with Amy's.

A parade of people began exiting the secured area. Linney searched the faces. She'd dismissed the slightly built man with rimmed glasses and a battered and bruised face until she saw him wave and start hurrying toward them.

He extended a hand toward Cutter. "I'm Bill Gibbons."

"Cutter Martin. Good to have you here."

"And I'm Linney," she said extending her hand after the men had finished their greetings. "You can't know how much I appreciate your coming to Houston, Dr. Gibbons."

"Call me Bill, and I should never have left."

"Are you from here?" she asked.

"No, but I was here last week." He rubbed his hand over his bruised and swollen face. "This is compliments of Dane."

"Last Friday? The day Amy drowned?"

"Yes." He glanced around. "I'd like to go somewhere more private to talk."

"Absolutely," Cutter said. "Is this all your luggage?"

"This is it." The doctor tugged on the handle of his wheeled overnighter.

"We can go to my house in Green's Harbor," Linney said. "There's an excellent deli nearby where we can get soup and sandwiches to go."

"Whatever you like," he said. "I'm not hungry."

Neither was Linney, but if the traffic was bad, it could take them an hour to get to her house and she didn't want the conversation cut short by anyone's wanting to go out to lunch.

They hurried through the double doors and to the parking lot where Cutter had left the rental car. He made them stand back while he checked the vehicle and then started the engine.

In spite of the argument they'd had last night. In spite of the strain between them that spiked the air with tension. In spite of it all, he was still heroic and protective.

Bill leaned over and opened the door for her. "Cutter obviously knows the enemy well. He's a real man. I like him."

"Yeah. Me, too." In spite of it all.

LINNEY'S BREAKFAST NOOK was the perfect place to hold what Cutter saw as an informal interrogation session. The small table made it cozy, the view of the garden pond with its bubbling waterfall made it nonthreatening, and it was totally private.

"I have lots of questions," Cutter said, "and I'm sure Linney does, too. Maybe we could bypass some of them if we let you talk first and tell us about your relationship with Amy."

Bill pushed his glasses up the narrow bridge of his nose. "I'm an English professor at a small college near Baltimore. I met Amy when she took a night class that I was teaching."

"I didn't know Amy ever lived in Baltimore," Linney said. "When was that?"

"Almost five years ago. She was twenty-nine to my thirty-six."

Which wasn't the only difference between them. Though Cutter never measured a man by the way he looked, he could clearly see they were no picture-perfect match. Amy could have been a supermodel, while Bill could play the part of a stereotypical professor on a Saturday-morning cartoon show. The man was small and wiry, with a receding hairline and a serious lack of muscle definition.

"Was Amy married then?" he asked

"No, but I was. Amy had moved to Baltimore with a guy she'd met in a substance abuse clinic in Los Angeles. Once they'd been clean for a while, they decided they weren't compatible."

"But she stayed in Baltimore?" Cutter asked, trying to get a hold on this, but eager to move on to more pertinent details, like why this guy had gotten his lights put out by Dane Colley the day Amy Colley drowned.

"Amy was making good money as a hostess in one

of the city's most exclusive and pricey restaurants. The owner of the restaurant is the one who suggested she take an English grammar class."

"I take it the two of you got involved," Cutter said.

"Not at first, but after the semester was over she asked me to meet her for coffee. Then we started meeting once a week. The sessions got longer and longer, stretching into dinner on nights neither of us was working."

Linney folded her arms. "What did you have in common?"

"Nothing, but we talked about everything, frequently about her past. I tried to get her to go to counseling to help her get past the shame and guilt, even offered to pay for it, but she wouldn't take my money."

"Did she know you were married?" Linney asked.

"Yes, we talked about my disintegrating marriage as well. I knew I was wrong to keep seeing Amy, but I fell in love with her. The miracle was she fell in love with me, too. I was going to ask for a divorce so that Amy and I could get married, but my wife asked for one first."

"Then why didn't you marry Amy?" Linney asked. This time the desperation tugged at her voice. "Why did you let her move to Texas and marry a man who treated her like a punching bag?"

"My wife was diagnosed with cancer. I couldn't leave her to fight that on her own. Amy understood. She broke things off and moved back to Texas to be near her mother."

And that should have been the end of the story, Cutter thought. Evidently, it hadn't been. "So how did you get from there to here, from breaking up to getting pulverized?"

"My wife died a little less than a year ago. I initiated e-mail contact with Amy about six months after that. Had Amy been happy with Dane, I swear I would have backed out of her life. But she told me that Dane was abusive and that he'd threatened to kill her if she left him. She was convinced he meant it."

"And that's exactly what he did," Amy said. "Did she ask you to come for her last Friday?"

"No. She told me she was going to sneak out of the house with Julie on Friday morning and that they would drive to Baltimore." Bill wiped his right hand across his eyes. "I was afraid she wouldn't go through with it or that he'd find out somehow and stop her, so I came anyway."

"Dane was supposed to be teaching a class of new recruits last Friday morning from eight-thirty until noon," Cutter said, thinking aloud. "She probably figured it was the perfect time to make a break for it."

"I called her when I was just outside Houston to let her know I'd come for her. I arrived at her house a few minutes before nine."

"Was Dane around then?" Linney asked.

"No, Amy was loading everything in her car. I talked her into transferring her luggage to my car and escaping with me. I thought it would make it more difficult for him to follow her. Dane drove up before we finished rearranging the luggage."

"So much for his ironclad alibi," Cutter said.

"I knew he was lying." Linney's voice rose. "Did you keep copies of the e-mails Amy wrote you, saying that Dane abused her and that she was afraid he would kill her if she left him?"

"I've saved every e-mail Amy ever wrote me."

"Then you have to go with us to the police station," Linney insisted. "You have to tell Chief Prentiss exactly what you told us. And if he doesn't arrest Dane, then we'll go to the media. We have evidence. Someone has to believe us."

Bill buried his face in his hands. "It's my fault. It's

all my fault. I should have showed up at that house with a gun. I should have killed Dane that day when I had the chance."

Cutter walked over and patted the guy's stooped shoulders. "Don't go blaming yourself, buddy. Dane had likely been threatening Amy for years. You couldn't know he'd ever follow through on it and especially that very day."

In fact, if this was how it had all gone down, Dane's timing was downright insane. He'd attacked Bill Gibbons in the Colley house in front of Amy and apparently even his daughter.

Dane had to know there was a chance Bill would come back to Houston and testify against him.

"Amy begged me to leave when Dane showed up," Bill said. "I guess I did eventually, but to tell you the truth, I don't remember what happened. I remember tasting blood and the world going black, but I don't remember leaving Amy."

"You must have been knocked unconscious," Linney said.

"I guess. All I know is I woke up around noon in a hotel on the edge of town. I found this note on my bloody pillow." He took a crumpled, printed note from his pocket and pressed it flat against the table's surface.

I'm sorry, but please don't come back. You are only making things more difficult for me. I'm with the man I love.

Cutter would have bet his last dollar that Amy never lived to write that note.

DANE ADJUSTED THE BINOCULAR lenses for a better view as Cutter, Linney and Dr. Bill Gibbons got into the car. Dane had figured Linney was up to something and had been watching her house for the last half hour. He was parked a block away, but there was nothing to interfere with his scrutiny or his reasoning power.

He'd beaten the crap out of that little weasel. Who'd have ever thought the professor would have the balls to show up in Green's Harbor again? Linney Kingston had to be behind this, just as she'd been behind every stinking thing that had happened since Amy's death.

He sputtered curses as the threesome drove away, then turned the key in his ignition. The engine purred to life. Desperation ground inside him. He was not going to jail. Not for Amy. Not for Linney and not for some wounded SEAL who'd been forced back to his godforsaken Dobbin ranch.

The gloves were off. It was time to fight dirty. And no one did that better than Dane—unless it was Wesley Evans.

His partner had taught him the ropes and impressed on him two key facts: nothing spoke louder than force and dead men didn't talk.

Chapter Fifteen

Cutter made the call to Saul Prentiss, explaining that he and Linney were bringing in a credible witness with pertinent facts concerning Amy's drowning. Bill had agreed that it was better not to mention his name in advance.

The chief had promised to make time for them, but had shown a decided lack of enthusiasm for this latest development.

He'd probably already alerted Dane and his sidekick Wesley—the very reason they hadn't mentioned Bill's name. It would only give Dane time to work on his alibi and make it look as if Bill were lying. Or else he'd concoct some wild tale about how Bill had been the threat and Dane had been protecting Amy from him.

Linney saw Bill's testimony as indisputable evidence that the drowning hadn't been an accident. Cutter had his doubts. If your advance is going well, you are walking into an ambush. That from Murphy's laws of combat.

Bill was in the passenger seat next to Cutter. Linney was in the back. Bill turned to face Linney. "Did you go to the funeral?"

"I did."

"Where is she buried?" His voice was tinged in pain.

"Nearby actually, in Everlasting Gardens."

"I'd like to stop by there for a few minutes, if it's not too much trouble."

Cutter's first impulse was to put him off until after his interview with Saul Prentiss, but there was no telling what the mood of any of them would be then. The professor was clearly suffering. He deserved a quiet chance to say good-bye before he was thrust into the minefield of law-enforcement bureaucracy.

"No trouble at all," Cutter said. He turned at the corner, then took Oak Street left toward the cemetery.

"Is there somewhere we can stop and buy flowers? Pink gladiola. Amy loved pale pink gladiola."

"You must be the one who sent her that gladiola bouquet for her birthday last month," Linney said. "Twelve pale pink gladiola blossoms were delivered to the school. They came on a Friday but she left them there over the weekend. I figured then they weren't from Dane."

"No, I didn't send them."

Interesting. If not from Dane or Bill, Cutter had to wonder if there was yet another man in Amy's life.

"There's a flower shop a block from the cemetery," Linney said. "Slow down a bit, Cutter. It's…right there, with the green awning out front."

Cutter stopped and Bill went inside, returning a few minutes later with one white gladiola. "It was all they had," he said. "I'll find pink ones later."

The gates to the cemetery were open. Cutter drove through. "Can you find the gravesite, Linney, or should I stop at the guard office for directions?"

"I can find it. Take the first left, then keep left."

Cutter slowed to the fifteen-mile-per-hour speed limit, checking behind him to make certain they weren't being followed. It was a habit he'd developed after the first attempt on Linney's life.

One thing you could count on with Linney, life was never dull when she was around.

Memories of last night came crashing down on him like tumbling bricks. She'd hit him with her best shot and he was still staggering from the blow. There was just too damn much truth in the accusations she'd hurled his way.

She'd been a thrill a minute in San Diego. He'd fallen hard but that didn't change the fact that he was gung-ho about SEALs.

If she'd stayed to tell him good-bye, if she'd told him she loved him… Hell, even if they'd had a quickie marriage, he'd have still caught that flight to Virginia and gone on with his training. Gone on with his life.

Blaming her because he'd let her get away had been the easy way out. Not that there was anything easy about losing Linney.

Yet here he was doing it all over again.

"It's right there," Linney said, lowering her window and pointing to a gravesite with no headstone as yet, but adorned with a standing wreath of wilted red roses.

Cutter slowed and stopped a few yards from the grave. He scanned the area. There was activity in the southern corner of Everlasting Gardens, and a young couple was visiting a site about fifty yards from where Cutter was parked. Nothing set off any alarms.

Linney led the way, with Bill following at her heels. Cutter stayed a few steps behind. He hadn't known Amy and felt like an intruder, imposing on their grief.

"Pink gladiola," Linney said. "I wonder who left them. Surely not Dane."

Cutter focused on the blooms that had spurred Linney's surprise. Three blossoms were tucked beneath the wreath's stand. The palest of pink. No vase. No water. Fresh in spite of the climbing temperature.

"It could have been anyone," Bill said. "Amy attracted admirers the way flowers attract bees."

There was no jealousy in his tone. Just grief.

Bill fell to his knees and put his one flower on the center of the earth that covered the coffin. "I let you down, Amy. Over and over again. I let him hurt you. I let him kill you." His voice broke, and tears ran down his sallow cheeks. "I won't let you down this time."

Linney knelt beside him and put her hand on his arm. "We all let her down, Bill. But I have an idea how we can start making it up to her when this is over. I'll need your help."

"If it honors Amy, count me in."

Cutter turned to watch a car that had turned onto the curved section of roadway where they were parked. His muscles tensed, his senses sharpened. His hand went to the butt of his gun.

The car stopped and an elderly lady got out. Leaning on her cane, she walked to a nearby gravesite, hiked her long skirt a bit and took a seat on the headstone.

"We should be going," he said. He had a really bad feeling about this place.

THE WAITING AREA at the police station was noisy and smelled of stale cigarettes and scalded coffee. Fortunately, the chief didn't keep them waiting long. Saul eyed Bill suspiciously as they were introduced, then led the three of them through a maze of cubicles to his office.

"Guess we need one more spot," Saul said, acting as if clearing the morning newspaper from a metal folding chair was a major undertaking.

He dropped the newspaper into a gray metal trash can, rounded his desk and plopped into a black leather swivel chair. "Before we get started, you should know that we've officially reopened the investigation into Amy Colley's drowning."

Linney cut him no slack. "Have you arrested Dane?"

"No, and I'm not at liberty to discuss any other details of the investigation at this time. Now what is this about your having new evidence?"

"Dr. Gibbons is a long-time friend of Amy's," Cutter said. "He'd been in contact with her by e-mail and was in the Colley home last Friday morning, when she was still alive. I think you'll be interested in what he has to say."

That got the chief's full attention. He pulled his chair closer to the desk and flicked on the small black recorder at the left edge of his desk. "I'm assuming you have no problem with my taping this."

"None at all," Bill assured him.

"And you'll swear to what you're about to say under oath if it comes to that?"

"I'm looking forward to it."

"Then let's hear it."

Bill had just gotten to the part where he'd arrived at the Colley home on Friday morning when the door to the chief's office burst open. Wesley Evans stepped inside.

"I'm in a meeting, Wesley."

Wesley glared at Linney. "I can see that. This can't wait."

"Okay." The chief stood and started toward the door. "We'll talk in the hall."

"No. Let Linney and Cutter hear this. It will make their day."

Saul grabbed Wesley's arm. "We'll talk in the hallway."

Wesley jerked from the man's grasp. "Dane Colley is dead."

The chief went white.

"I found him out by his pool with a bullet from his own gun through his head. He killed himself. And the rest of you can all go straight to hell."

LINNEY TURNED THE KEY in the lock and opened her front door. She was numb, body and soul. So much had happened over the last few days. She'd poured everything she had into her quest for justice. She'd been determined that Dane would pay for Amy's death.

But not like this. Not without a trial. Not with questions left unanswered. Not with Dane a martyr to everyone who didn't know the real story.

But maybe it was better for Julie this way. She'd never have to face the man who'd killed her mother or risk becoming the new beneficiary of his abuse.

Linney kicked off her shoes as she stepped through the door. Cutter had wanted to come inside with her, but she'd insisted that he and Bill just drop her off. She didn't need protection with Dane dead.

She needed time to think. About Amy. About Dane. About Cutter.

Right now she needed a hot shower. She felt as if the stench of Amy's and even Dane's death clung to her skin. She went straight to her bedroom and slipped out of her clothes except for her bra and panties. Chilling shivers climbed her spine as she stepped into the bathroom. She had the eerie feeling that someone was watching her. The bizarre events of the last few days were taking their toll.

Her medicine cabinet stood open. An opened bottle of pills was on the counter next to the basin. She was sure she hadn't left it there.

Picking it up, she checked the label. OxyContin. The pain reliever wasn't even her prescription; it belonged to a friend who'd stayed with Linney for a few days following back surgery.

So who had opened the pill bottle today? Bill? Cutter?

The shower curtain jiggled. Linney's heart slammed against her chest. Someone was in the bathroom with her.

She turned and started to run. Footsteps sounded behind her, and she was knocked against the wall.

A rough hand clamped around her arm. "You can't leave now, Linney. We're about to party."

She turned and met a burning, accusing stare. "Wesley."

"Yeah, it's me." His grip tightened. "Just you and me. No hero to save you now. We're finally alone."

Chapter Sixteen

Fear rattled through Linney as if giant hands were shaking her. This was all a mistake. She had to make Wesley see that. "Amy was my friend. I only wanted a full investigation. I didn't cause Dane's death."

"Ah, but you did. If you'd just stayed out of things, I wouldn't have had to kill him."

Conflicting thoughts battled in Linney's mind. "You didn't kill Dane. He committed suicide. It wasn't your fault. It was no one's fault but his own. He killed Amy."

Wesley yanked her back into the bedroom. "You think you have it all figured out, don't you? You think you know it all, but you're just a naive little fool."

His words pushed all the wrong buttons. She took a deep breath and brought her knee up to his groin with enough force that he yelped in pain.

"You bitch."

She was about to knee him again when she felt the sharp prick in her arm and caught a glimpse of the needle Wesley had plunged into her flesh. She was being drugged. She had to get away.

Her breath came in jagged gasps and she forced all her strength into a fierce head butt that left her reeling. Wesley's grip held tight.

"Party's started, Linney. You may as well relax and go with the flow. The good thing is you won't remember a thing when you wake up. Oh, wait. My mistake. You won't wake up."

He started to laugh, a maddening sound that grated on her every nerve. She shuddered uncontrollably until the fury and the raucous noise faded into the purplish, hazy background that coated her mind.

The OxyContin.

"You're the one who opened the pills," she said.

"Yes, and it was a brilliant move on my part. The first thing a good detective looks for in a case of overdose is the origin of the drug. This one was right in your medicine cabinet, obviously shared with you by a friend. Nice that I snooped the other day when I dropped off the pictures of Amy for you to enjoy."

Wesley dragged her to the bed. Oh, God, was he going to rape her, too? She was already undressed, wearing nothing but a bra and her panties. She tried to cover herself with her hands.

"Don't worry. I don't want sex with the likes of you. Besides, fresh sperm on your dead body would spoil my perfect murder and break my perfect record."

She didn't want to die. She had to find a way out of this. "Please, don't do this, Wesley. You won't get away with it. Cutter will find out and he'll kill you."

"I'm not afraid of Cutter. All that hero talk is a bunch of military hogwash."

Linney grew dizzy and the room started to spin. She was falling or being dropped. She landed on something soft. Her bed. Good. She'd close her eyes and—

No. Wesley was going to kill her. She had to stay alert, had to stop him.

"Here you go, you little trouble-causing tramp. A few sips of whiskey. Alcohol will intensify the effects of crushed oxycodone in the bloodstream. And it's always nice to have a little booze in the system when the autopsy is conducted."

She gagged but the liquid kept coming. Wesley lifted her head and she swallowed. The burn seemed to set her throat and stomach on fire.

Her eyes closed. The purple in her mind was streaked with silver. There was music. She was dancing with Cutter on a moonlit beach.

"I love you, Cutter. I've always loved you. I always will."

The streaks of silver turned to an inky liquid that was spilling over Wesley's head. "Why? Why kill me?"

"Because you were never going to let up until the truth came out. I couldn't let that happen. Amy got what she deserved. No one walks all over me."

The whiskey started coming at her again, a choking burn that spilled over her lips and tore at her throat. Wesley's face began to fade in and out like frightening shadows skulking across a ceiling.

Stay focused.

"I'm trying, Cutter. I'm trying."

Only Cutter wasn't there. It was just her and a madman floating in a field of black.

"I'M GLAD DANE'S DEAD. I came here intending to kill him myself, but I don't know if I could have ever gone through with it."

Cutter took his eyes off the road and looked at the bespectacled professor with the thinning hair and mild manners, amazed again by the intensity of emotion that surged within him.

"You really loved Amy, didn't you?"

"Yes. We were meant to be together. The timing was just never right for us."

Like the timing between Cutter and Linney when they'd run into each other in San Diego. The passion, sex and exploding emotions had been scorching hot. But she was right. It wouldn't have mattered what either of them had said or done at the time.

He was off to be a SEAL and nothing could have stopped him. Looking back, he knew he wouldn't change that. The SEALs had made him who he was. And, even injured, he knew he'd never be happy living life on the sidelines.

The experiences over the last few days when he'd been shoved back into the fight of right against wrong, good against evil had proved that. He loved the ranch. He was a cowboy to his soul. But he wasn't a rancher, at least not yet.

Maybe it was the same for Amy. She'd married Al. It hadn't worked, but it had given her a taste of a lifestyle that she apparently wanted more of. From the poor side of the tracks to a life of luxury. If that's what she wanted, she should have it.

"You're right about timing," Cutter said. "It makes all the difference between happily ever after and losing out."

"The miracle was that someone as beautiful and loving as Amy could ever even be attracted to someone like me."

"There's more to love than looks," Cutter said.

"Yeah, I guess Wesley Evans proved that."

"I'm not sure where you got that from."

"Let's face it," Bill said. "Wesley has a lot more of what the women at the college call the hunk factor than I do. And he was here for her when I wasn't. Amy mentioned more than once that he'd stuck up for her and protected her when Dane was on one of his abusive warpaths."

The comments surprised Cutter. "You never mentioned anything about Wesley before."

"Didn't I? I don't know what I've said. Finding out that Amy's dead has left me almost in shock. But Amy did mention once that she thought Wesley was falling in love with her. That's another reason she felt she had to get away. She didn't want to hurt him."

"And yet he stood by Dane when the cause of Amy's death was considered questionable."

The facts didn't add up. If Wesley loved Amy, he should have been furious with Dane if he thought Dane might have killed her, not defending him.

"Do you think Wesley knew that Amy was running away to be with you?"

"I doubt that she would have told him," Bill said, "but Dane may have filled him in after the fact. After he knocked me unconscious and dumped me at that hotel in town."

Or maybe Dane hadn't been the one to drive Bill to the hotel. He would have had to go back to the class he was teaching.

But he could have called Wesley into service. Wesley Evans, the trusted partner.

Wesley Evans, the rejected would-be lover.

Apprehension pitted in Cutter's gut. As he drove, he grabbed his cell phone and punched in Linney's number. The incessant ringing seemed interminable. Finally, her voice mail picked up.

Cutter gunned his engine and swerved into the exit lane.

"Is there a problem?" Bill asked.

"I hope not, Prof." But his instincts for danger shouted that there was.

WESLEY STARED into Linney Kingston's eyes. Her pupils had contracted until they were little more than drifting pinpricks in a field of speckled green. Her arms flopped about like a dying fish when she tried to lift them. Her breathing was slow, her skin clammy.

He wasn't sorry to see Linney go this way, but he was glad Amy had died quickly. Had it been slow like this, he might not have been able to go through with killing her.

He hadn't wanted to kill her, but she'd pushed him too far. He was the one who'd protected her when Dane flew off the handle. He was the one who remembered her birthday and made her laugh. He was the one who'd stood by while her marriage with Dane ran its rocky course.

Amy had never even mentioned Bill to Wesley. The first he'd known the man existed was when Dane found them running away together and practically killed the man. When Dane had explained the situation and asked Wesley to dump the professor in a cheap motel, it was as if every cell in Wesley's body had been sucked into a state of rage. He'd done as Dane had asked—after Dane had gone back to the class he was teaching.

After Wesley had exploded and drowned Amy.

Even Dane had never suspected Wesley of killing Amy. Not until Wesley had been forced to kill him to make the trail go cold, to put an end to any possibility of the truth coming out.

"Here's to you, Linney." He raised the almost-empty glass of whiskey. "Chalk up Dane's murder and your own to your prying and snooping."

Wesley finished the whiskey off himself. There were enough drugs and alcohol in Linney now to ensure the desired autopsy findings. Massive amounts of pain reliever and measurable amounts of alcohol in the bloodstream.

She'd been behaving irrationally ever since her friend's death. Obvious depression. No one would question the findings. Not even Cutter Martin.

One more syringe of crumbled meds dissolved in

liquid should do it. Her eyes fluttered as if she knew what was coming. He positioned the needle to deliver the killing dose.

"Say hello to Amy for me. Tell her what a fool she was to choose Bill Gibbons over me."

Linney was so out of it that she didn't whimper when he sank the needle into her flesh and the drug flowed effortlessly into her veins.

Chapter Seventeen

Linney drifted in the purple haze. Wesley was in the vapor as well. She heard him from time to time, but it was as if he were too far away for his words to register. She tried to open her eyes. The lids were too heavy. She was dying from the pills and whiskey that floated with her in the miasma.

A new voice shattered the murky haze. Cutter? It couldn't be. She forced her eyes to open. He appeared for a second and then his shape became fuzzy.

"Move away from Linney or I'll put a bullet through your head."

Linney was jerked from the bed. The movement felt like ice dripping into her pores. The shock pushed her out of the haze. Her eyes fluttered and finally fixed on Wesley's shoulder and the side of his ear.

"Go ahead, shoot. But it will be Linney you kill."

Wesley was using her as a shield. That meant Cutter was here. The mind-numbing fog tried to pull her back inside it, but she fought to stay alert. Voices seemed to be coming at her from all directions. Orders. Curses.

Cutter was here. She needed to get to him, but Wesley was holding her back. She tried to push away from him, but his grip tightened. He grabbed a handful of her hair and yanked until it felt as if her brain were being torn from her skull.

She saw his eyes. Black evil lights glowing through the fog. She had to put them out. Calling on all her strength, she managed to free her hands and shoot them toward his face. The tips of her index fingers delved into the dark iniquitous pits of his eyeballs.

Wesley knocked her away. Gunfire blasted through the room, and hot, sticky crimson spewed like lava.

"It's okay, baby. I've got you. I've got you and I'm never going to let you go."

Cutter took her in his arms and they were back once again, dancing on the golden sand.

He sounded as if he was crying, but then his sobs were drowned out by the crashing waves that swept her off the shore into the darkness.

CUTTER WAS A TOTAL WRECK as the paramedics loaded Linney into the ambulance. Her pulse was weak, and her blood pressure was dropping fast. But she couldn't die. Not this way. Not now. He wouldn't let her. He started to climb into the back of the ambulance with her.

"Sorry, buddy. You'll have to come in your own car. We're only allowed to carry the injured."

He was about to tell them what they could do with their rules when Saul Prentiss walked up. Cutter hadn't even seen him arrive on the scene since he'd left Bill to deal with the cops who'd answered his 9-1-1 call.

"Let him go with you," the chief said. "Police orders."

"Yes, sir."

Saul reached up to close the door behind him. "We'll talk later. I hope Linney makes it. She's quite a woman."

"You're right." Cutter swallowed hard. She'd always been quite a woman. He'd just never admitted to himself how terrific she was or how much he needed her.

He knew how to fight. He knew how to survive. Finally, he'd learned to love.

Please, God, don't let it be too late.

One week later

"LAND SAKES, I've half a mind to throttle you, Cutter Martin, for not calling me in Alaska and telling me what was going on. I'd have been on the first plane home."

"And wanting to run the show," Cutter said.

"Like aunt, like nephew," Linney said.

Merlee chuckled as she spooned a generous helping of the freshly made banana pudding into a bowl and passed it to Linney. "Are you sure you're okay, Linney? I mean, you look great, but you don't want to overdo it."

"I'm fine, thanks to Cutter." And she was, though it had been touch and go for a few hours. She'd been too out of it to know how close she'd come to dying, but once she was out of danger the doctor had filled her in on the details.

Cutter had stayed with her in the hospital and had insisted on bringing her to the ranch to recuperate when she'd been released. He'd been a terrific nurse, but that was it. They hadn't shared a room. They hadn't made love.

And there had been no mention of the angry accusations they'd hurled at each other about the reasons they'd both gone their separate ways six years ago. In fact, Cutter had seemed preoccupied most of the week and had spent hours on the telephone.

It was as if he were pulling away from her emotionally even while he was pampering her to the point that she was ready to rebel. She no longer needed a nurse. She needed Cutter. All of him. She couldn't settle for less.

Merlee finished serving the banana pudding. This was her homecoming dinner, but she'd insisted on making the dessert. She'd missed her kitchen, she claimed. Cutter had done the rest, most of it on the outdoor grill. Between the two of them, Linney was lucky they let her make a salad and set the table.

"You must have been terrified when Wesley kept shooting those drugs into you," Merlee said.

"Probably, but luckily I don't remember most of it. I do remember looking up and seeing Cutter. It was a spectacular rescue."

"Cutter's a natural-born hero," Merlee said. Her pride in him shone in her bright blue eyes and the deep smile lines that crinkled her pudgy face.

"I didn't do it alone," Cutter said. "Linney's the one who nearly put Wesley's eyes out."

"But you saved my life three times in as many days," Linney reminded him.

"And all three times it was that Wesley guy who was behind it," Merlee said. "And to think he was a cop."

"A dirty cop who'd killed his partner's wife and his partner," Cutter said. "Guess it takes all kinds."

"I was so sure that Dane had killed Amy," Linney admitted. "It would never have occurred to me that Wesley was the guilty one."

"And it looks like he'll live to go to trial," Cutter said. "I had a call from Saul Prentiss this morning. He says Wesley's backing down from the confessions he made when he thought he was dying from the bullet I put into him, but he's sure they still have enough evidence to get a conviction."

"But poor Julie," Merlee said. "Both her parents dead. Thank goodness she has her grandmother."

"That's the rest of the good news," Cutter said. "I haven't even had a chance to tell Linney this. Bill called while I was taking the steaks off the grill. He got the DNA test results back today. Julie is actually his daughter."

"That's terrific." Linney's eyes filled with tears. She'd been praying so hard that that would be the case. "Bill must be ecstatic."

"So much so he could barely talk."

Merlee waved her empty spoon. "The professor is the father. I must have missed something."

"He never knew it," Linney said. "Amy moved away when his wife got sick and Bill went back to her. Evidently, Amy was pregnant with Bill's child when she married Dane."

"This is some soap opera," Merlee said. "I guess all's well that ends well." She waved an empty spoon at Cutter. "You make sure this all ends well."

"Yes, ma'am. I'll give it my best shot."

The talk went back to the Alaska adventure as they finished their dessert. When Merlee began to gather the empty bowls, Linney jumped up to help.

"You just keep your seat," Merlee said. "I'm looking forward to cleaning my own kitchen after being waited on hand and foot for two weeks."

"In that case, Linney and I will go outside and catch the sunset." Cutter gave a Merlee a conspiratorial wink.

Linney had no idea what they'd cooked up, but if it was more pampering, she was going to have to draw the line.

"Are you up for a drive down to the swimming hole?" Cutter asked when they reached the porch. "Not to swim—unless you want to swim."

"Not if you have something more exciting in mind," she baited.

He didn't bite. It was as if sex were the furthest thing from his mind these days. He was moving on with his life. It was probably time she went back to Green's Harbor and moved ahead with hers as well.

Neither of them talked as Cutter drove to the swimming hole and parked at the end of the rutted road. They walked side by side to the edge of the water. Images of the passion that had exploded the last time they were here haunted Linney's mind.

She sat down on a carpet of sweet-smelling grass, crossing her legs. Cutter didn't join her, but leaned against the slender trunk of a nearby pine tree.

"I've been doing a lot of thinking this week," he said.

"About what?" she asked, though she wasn't sure she wanted to know.

"About what to do with the rest of my life. Originally, I thought I'd be able to take a regular civilian job and make a go of it, but I realize now that that won't work for me."

Linney's breath grew jagged. If this was where he told her he was moving on, she'd just as soon skip this part. "You don't have to explain your decisions to me."

"I want to. Working with you to find Amy's killer and keep you safe inspired my decisions. All this week I've talked to several of my former special ops teammates who are pretty much in the same boat I'm in. Out of the service, but still looking for their niche."

"So have you found your niche, Cutter?"

"I think so. I'm going to start a protection/investigative business. I want to handle cases the law can't solve because of limited manpower or because their hands are tied by rules and restrictions. I've hired one guy to join me. It'll be just the two of us for starters."

Her throat tightened. "Where will your work be located?"

"The Double M Ranch. Aunt Merlee is thrilled with that. She keeps reminding me that it's actually my ranch any time I take control so she can play more."

"I didn't realize the ranch belonged to you."

"The land was passed down to my dad and Uncle Hank from my grandparents. I'm the only Martin descendant, so when Uncle Hank died it went to me, with the assurance that Merlee would live here as long as she chose. I wouldn't have it any other way."

"It sounds as if you have it all worked out."

"Not quite." Cutter shoved his hands into his pockets. "It's like this, Linney. I realize you need a lot more luxury than the ranch offers, and I'm willing to go along with—"

"Wait a minute. Who ever said I was looking for luxury?"

"You wanted security when you married Al. And that settlement seems awful important to you—not that you shouldn't get it. It's rightfully yours."

"Security isn't luxury, and frankly living like the rich and famous isn't all it's cracked up to be."

"That's nice to know."

"And I never planned to spend that settlement on a lavish lifestyle. I just thought I could use some of the vast funds Al's accumulated to actually do some good."

She swatted at a mosquito that buzzed her right ear. "I'm made some decisions, too, Cutter. If I ever actually get that money, I'm going to use it to build and operate battered women's centers across the state. I've talked to Bill. He's agreed to take a year's sabbatical—when and if the project comes to fruition—so that he can help me get it off the ground."

"Then you don't want to live in a mansion with a staff of dozens?"

"Heaven forbid. I had enough of that with Al."

"Whew!" Cutter dropped down beside her. "But that does present another problem."

"A problem?"

"I don't think the ranch house is big enough for all the kids you said you want. We'll have to add on."

Add on to his house. For her kids. Linney's heart began to pound. Her stomach churned. "Is this a proposal?"

"That was my intention." He pulled a ring from his pocket and got on one knee. "Will you marry me, Linney? Will you live on the ranch with me and be my wife and the mother of as many children as your heart desires and your body can stand to have?"

Tears filled her eyes. She'd never wanted anything more, but not like this. She shook her head. "Not if that's all there is to the proposal."

Cutter grimaced. "How did I screw up?"

"You haven't said 'I love you.' You've never once said 'I love you.'"

His lips parted in a devastating smile. He rose from his knee and pulled her into his arms. "I'm a man of action, not words. But I love you, Linney, more than I could tell you if I had a million words at my command. I plan to spend the rest of my life showing you how much."

"And I love you, too, Cutter. I always will."

He twirled the sparkling diamond ring. "Now will you marry me or do I have to just throw you over my shoulder and run off with you like the Neanderthal I am?"

She slipped her arms around his neck. "Yes. The answer is yes."

And then Cutter kissed her and did what he did best. After all, he was a man of action.

* * * * *

Celebrate 60 years of pure
reading pleasure with Harlequin®!
Silhouette® Romantic Suspense is celebrating
with the glamour-filled, adrenaline-charged series
LOVE IN 60 SECONDS
starting in April 2009.
Six stories that promise to bring the
glitz of Las Vegas, the danger of revenge,
the mystery of a missing diamond, family scandals
and ripped-from-the-headlines intrigue.
Get your heart racing
as love happens in sixty seconds!

Enjoy a sneak peek of
USA TODAY bestselling author
Marie Ferrarella's
THE HEIRESS'S 2-WEEK AFFAIR
Available April 2009
from Silhouette® Romantic Suspense.

Eight years ago Matt Shaffer had vanished out of Natalie Rothchild's life, leaving behind a one-line note tucked under a pillow that had grown cold: *I'm sorry, but this just isn't going to work.*

That was it. No explanation, no real indication of remorse. The note had been as clinical and compassionless as an eviction notice, which, in effect, it had been, Natalie thought as she navigated through the morning traffic. Matt had written the note to evict her from his life.

She'd spent the next two weeks crying, breaking down without warning as she walked down the street, or as she sat staring at a meal she couldn't bring herself to eat.

Candace, she remembered with a bittersweet pang, had tried to get her to go clubbing in order to get her to forget about Matt.

She'd turned her twin down, but she did get her act together. If Matt didn't think enough of their relationship to try to contact her, to try to make her understand why he'd changed so radically from lover to stranger, then to hell with him. He was dead to her, she resolved. And he'd remained that way.

Until twenty minutes ago.

The adrenaline in her veins kept mounting.

Natalie focused on her driving. Vegas in the daylight wasn't nearly as alluring, as magical and glitzy as it was after dark. Like an aging woman best seen in soft lighting, Vegas's imperfections were all visible in the daylight. Natalie supposed that was why people like her sister didn't like to get up until noon. They lived for the night.

Except that Candace could no longer do that.

The thought brought a fresh, sharp ache with it.

"Damn it, Candy, what a waste," Natalie murmured under her breath.

She pulled up before the Janus casino. One of the three valets currently on duty came to life and made a beeline for her vehicle.

"Welcome to the Janus," the young attendant said cheerfully as he opened her door with a flourish.

"We'll see," she replied solemnly.

As he pulled away with her car, Natalie looked up at the casino's logo. Janus was the Roman god with two faces, one pointed toward the past, the other facing the future. It struck her as rather ironic, given what she was doing here, seeking out someone from her past in order to get answers so that the future could be settled.

The moment she entered the casino, the Vegas phenomena took hold. It was like stepping into a world where time did not matter or even make an appearance. There was only a sense of "now."

Because in Natalie's experience she'd discovered that bartenders knew the inner workings of any establishment they worked for better than anyone else, she made her way to the first bar she saw within the casino.

The bartender in attendance was a gregarious man in his early forties. He had a quick, sexy smile, which was probably one of the main reasons he'd been hired. His name tag identified him as Kevin.

Moving to her end of the bar, Kevin asked, "What'll it be, pretty lady?"

"Information." She saw a dubious look cross his brow. To counter that, she took out her badge. Granted she wasn't here in an official capacity, but Kevin didn't need to know that. "Were you on duty last night?"

Kevin began to wipe the gleaming black surface of the bar. "You mean during the gala?"

"Yes."

The smile gracing his lips was a satisfied one. Last night had obviously been profitable for him, she judged. "I caught an extra shift."

She took out Candace's photograph and carefully placed it on the bar. "Did you happen to see this woman there?"

The bartender glanced at the picture. Mild interest turned to recognition. "You mean Candace Rothchild? Yeah, she was here, loud and brassy as always. But not for long," he added, looking rather disappointed. There was always a circus when Candace was around, Natalie thought. "She and the boss had at it and then he had our head of security escort her out."

She latched onto the first part of his statement. "They argued? About what?"

He shook his head. "Couldn't tell you. Too far away for anything but body language," he confessed.

"And the head of security?" she asked.

"He got her to leave."

She leaned in over the bar. "Tell me about him."

"Don't know much," the bartender admitted. "Just that his name's Matt Shaffer. Boss flew him in from L.A., where he was head of security for Montgomery Enterprises."

There was no avoiding it, she thought darkly. She was going to have to talk to Matt. The thought left her cold. "Do you know where I can find him right now?"

Kevin glanced at his watch. "He should be in his office. On the second floor, toward the rear." He gave her the numbers of the rooms where the monitors that kept watch over the casino guests as they tried their luck against the house were located.

Taking out a twenty, she placed it on the bar. "Thanks for your help."

Kevin slipped the bill into his vest pocket. "Any time, lovely lady," he called after her. "Any time."

She debated going up the stairs, then decided on the elevator. The car that took her up to the second floor was empty. Natalie stepped out of the elevator, looked around to get her bearings and then walked toward the rear of the floor.

"Into the Valley of Death rode the six hundred," she silently recited, digging deep for a line from a poem by Tennyson. Wrapping her hand around a brass handle, she opened one of the glass doors and walked in.

The woman whose desk was closest to the door looked up. "You can't come in here. This is a restricted area."

Natalie already had her ID in her hand and held it up. "I'm looking for Matt Shaffer," she told the woman.

God, even saying his name made her mouth go dry. She was supposed to be over him, to have moved on with her life. What happened?

The woman began to answer her. "He's—"

"Right here."

The deep voice came from behind her. Natalie felt every single nerve ending go on tactical alert at the same moment that all the hairs at the back of her neck stood up. Eight years had passed, but she would have recognized his voice anywhere.

* * * * *

*Why did Matt Shaffer leave heiress-turned-cop
Natalie Rothchild?
What does he know about the death of Natalie's
twin sister?
Come and meet these two reunited lovers and learn
the secrets of the Rothchild family in
THE HEIRESS'S 2-WEEK AFFAIR
by USA TODAY bestselling author
Marie Ferrarella.
The first book in Silhouette® Romantic Suspense's
wildly romantic new continuity,
LOVE IN 60 SECONDS!
Available April 2009.*

CELEBRATE
60 YEARS
OF PURE READING PLEASURE
WITH HARLEQUIN®!

Look for Silhouette®
Romantic Suspense in April!

Love In 60 Seconds
Bright lights. Big city. Hearts in overdrive.

Silhouette® Romantic Suspense is celebrating
Harlequin's 60th Anniversary with six stories that
promise to bring readers the glitz of Las Vegas,
the danger of revenge, the mystery of a missing
diamond, and family scandals.

Look for the first title, *The Heiress's 2-Week Affair*
by *USA TODAY* bestselling author
Marie Ferrarella, on sale in April!

His 7-Day Fiancée by **Gail Barrett**	May
The 9-Month Bodyguard by **Cindy Dees**	June
Prince Charming for 1 Night by **Nina Bruhns**	July
Her 24-Hour Protector by **Loreth Anne White**	August
5 minutes to Marriage by **Carla Cassidy**	September

---

www.eHarlequin.com　　　　　SRS60BPA

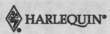

The Inside Romance newsletter has a NEW look for the new year!

Same great content, brand-new look!

The Inside Romance newsletter is a FREE quarterly newsletter highlighting our upcoming series releases and promotions!

Click on the Inside Romance link on the front page of **www.eHarlequin.com** or e-mail us at insideromance@harlequin.ca to sign up to receive your FREE newsletter today!

You can also subscribe by writing to us at: HARLEQUIN BOOKS Attention: Customer Service Department P.O. Box 9057, Buffalo, NY 14269-9057

Please allow 4-6 weeks for delivery of the first issue by mail.

IRNNEW09

REQUEST YOUR FREE BOOKS!

2 FREE NOVELS PLUS 2 FREE GIFTS!

HARLEQUIN®
INTRIGUE®

Breathtaking Romantic Suspense

YES! Please send me 2 FREE Harlequin Intrigue® novels and my 2 FREE gifts (gifts are worth about $10). After receiving them, if I don't wish to receive any more books, I can return the shipping statement marked "cancel." If I don't cancel, I will receive 6 brand-new novels every month and be billed just $4.24 per book in the U.S. or $4.99 per book in Canada. That's a savings of close to 15% off the cover price! It's quite a bargain! Shipping and handling is just 25¢ per book*. I understand that accepting the 2 free books and gifts places me under no obligation to buy anything. I can always return a shipment and cancel at any time. Even if I never buy another book from Harlequin, the two free books and gifts are mine to keep forever.

182 HDN EEZ7   382 HDN EEZK

Name	(PLEASE PRINT)

Address	Apt. #

City	State/Prov.	Zip/Postal Code

Signature (if under 18, a parent or guardian must sign)

Mail to the **Harlequin Reader Service:**
IN U.S.A.: P.O. Box 1867, Buffalo, NY 14240-1867
IN CANADA: P.O. Box 609, Fort Erie, Ontario L2A 5X3

Not valid to current subscribers of Harlequin Intrigue books.

**Are you a current subscriber of Harlequin Intrigue books
and want to receive the larger-print edition?
Call 1-800-873-8635 today!**

* Terms and prices subject to change without notice. Prices do not include applicable taxes. Sales tax applicable in N.Y. Canadian residents will be charged applicable provincial taxes and GST. Offer not valid in Quebec. This offer is limited to one order per household. All orders subject to approval. Credit or debit balances in a customer's account(s) may be offset by any other outstanding balance owed by or to the customer. Please allow 4 to 6 weeks for delivery. Offer available while quantities last.

Your Privacy: Harlequin is committed to protecting your privacy. Our Privacy Policy is available online at www.eHarlequin.com or upon request from the Reader Service. From time to time we make our lists of customers available to reputable third parties who may have a product or service of interest to you. If you would prefer we not share your name and address, please check here. ☐

You're invited to join our Tell Harlequin Reader Panel!

By joining our new reader panel you will:

- Receive Harlequin® books—they are FREE and yours to keep with no obligation to purchase anything!
- Participate in fun online surveys
- Exchange opinions and ideas with women just like you
- Have a say in our new book ideas and help us publish the best in women's fiction

In addition, you will have a chance to win great prizes and receive special gifts! See Web site for details. Some conditions apply. Space is limited.

To join, visit us at
www.TellHarlequin.com.

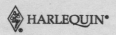

INTRIGUE®

COMING NEXT MONTH

Available April 14, 2009

#1125 SHOTGUN BRIDE by B.J. Daniels
Whitehorse, Montana: The Corbetts
A former Texas Ranger is not prepared to fall for a blue-eyed Montana cowgirl who has had enough of heartbreak. When her troubling past leads to her abduction, is he ready to ride to her rescue?

#1126 CRIMINALLY HANDSOME by Cassie Miles
Kenner County Crime Unit
A terrifying vision sends a frightened psychic into the protective arms of a skeptical CSI expert. To catch a killer, they will need to work together—closely.

#1127 BABY BLING by Elle James
Diamonds and Daddies
Two months ago, Houston's shipping tycoon slept with the one woman he should have left alone—his assistant and friend. Now he needs her help to stop terrorists, and she needs to tell him she is pregnant!

#1128 RESCUING THE VIRGIN by Patricia Rosemoor
The McKenna Legacy
An undercover special agent is shocked when he discovers a beautiful American woman trapped by the human-trafficking ring he is trying to bring down. Can he save her and bring the mastermind behind the scheme to justice?

#1129 A STRANGER'S BABY by Kerry Connor
With the help of the handsome man next door, she is unraveling the sinister truth behind the one-night stand that left her pregnant and alone. Now that someone is threatening her baby and safety, can they find out the truth before it is too late?

#1130 BULLETPROOF TEXAS by Kay Thomas
To extract cancer-eating bacteria from a flooding cave, a research scientist accepts the help of a laid-back caving guide. But a psychopathic competitor decides this potential cure shouldn't see the light of day— and is willing to kill anyone who gets in the way.

HICNMBPA0309